If I Say No

A Collection of What If's

A Zimbell House Anthology

ZIMBELL HOUSE
PUBLISHING
UNION LAKE, MICHIGAN

© 2018 Zimbell House Publishing

Published in the United States by Zimbell House Publishing
http://www.ZimbellHousePublishing.com

All Rights Reserved

Trade Paper ISBN: 978-1-947210-37-0
Kindle ISBN: 978-1-947210-38-7
Digital ISBN: 978-1-947210-39-4
Library of Congress Control Number: 2018904267

First Edition: April/2018
10 9 8 7 6 5 4 3 2 1

A Zimbell House Anthology
If I Say No
A Collection of What If's

Acknowledgments

Zimbell House Publishing would like to thank all those that contributed to this anthology. We chose to showcase four new voices that best represented our vision for this work.

We would also like to thank our Zimbell House team for all their hard work and dedication to these projects.

Contents

Had I Said No

Gene J. Parola

Queen Ka'ahumanu squinted from the shady porch of her imported American house. She had slipped from the pile of sitting mats to sprawl on the large one covering the floor.

She watched as Lord Byron's frigate stood out from Honolulu, its task of returning the bodies of the Hawaiian King and Queen finished.

Of course, we are all dead now. But in the tradition of the Kanaka Maoli, the Polynesian 'true people,' we have become aumakua, spiritual advisors, for those still living. And we remember.

I am John Young, born in Leicestershire, England and was a bos'un on an American ship when old King Kamehameha kidnapped me while I was ashore filling water casks.

I became Olohana finally, the most trusted adviser to the old chief ... perhaps because I made him rich. But also, because I knew the way of the strangers who came to these shores, and I protected him from them. I was the last to exchange breath with him when he died, and the Queen is jealous of that, so has not sought much of my council since. Boki is always resentful of me because I know his tricks and his foreign friends.

Listen and watch as they try to right the balance of their Kingless Kingdom amid an external threat.

The Queen lay on the mat.

The boy passed this great woman her lighted pipe, then took up the fly whisk and resumed his endless task. The pet pig came out to join her mistress in the shade, flopping down noisily at the royal feet.

It had been a busy few days—a week, the missionaries would call it.

The royal bodies were being processed Kanaka ali'i style. A messy job after such a long delay. Possession of the elegant coffins supplied by the British government for the visiting royals was now a subject of jealous argument.

The size of the frigate's sails were diminishing in the distance.

"I'm no longer hampered by the young fool," she mused, pulling deeply on the pipe. "I should have killed him long ago. Vancouver and his stupid British 'royal-line' advice." She expelled the smoke vigorously from both nostrils.

"Simply being a King's son had not made him a King."

"I could have said no to the lot of them. I should have said it then."

A dog barked down the dusty road near the fort. A man had emerged from one of the ramshackle grass-hut taverns and plodded toward the royal residence.

It was the hottest part of the day, and almost everybody, Kanaka, and haole alike sought shade and a breath of trade-wind breeze if possible. It was also a time of fewer witnesses to royal movements and with fewer cocked ears.

"What did Boki want," she wondered aloud. "He will use all the wiles of his great speaking skill. Only my uncle could best him in the contests. It may become an oratorical debate today."

Boki was a handsome Kanaka chief, governor of the island of Oahu, respected by most of the Council of Chiefs and a regular antagonizer of the Queen.

She spoke quickly, and the gate guards lowered the crossed kahilis before her arrogant visitor had a chance to brush them aside. She debated about standing to greet him, then decided that simply sitting up was enough. She twisted her more than ample torso around, wiggled back onto the mats, feet stretched out before her. Toward him.

But he had stopped outside the gate. He lowered his head, extended his hand, palm down, at arm's reach.

"Aloha, ma'i, my sister," he crooned.

"A cousin at most," she responded. "No nearer, I'm sure."

"You are always correct, cousin. But you are not always right." He entered the gate and walked slowly toward the seated monarch.

With a raised hand she stopped his progress. "And you are here to decide if my latest decision is the 'right' one?"

Boki knew, long before the missionaries came pronouncing everything the Kanaka did as a sin, that he could only sin against the teaching of his own religion. Most Kanaka did not know this important distinction. The sin the missionary experienced was in seeing the naked breasts of a wahine was actually in his own lustful imagination, not in her comfortable undress. This was only one of the disagreements he had with the newcomers and their multitudes of 'sins.'

Early on, he had understood the advantages of the white man's trading practices. The idea of profit was easy to understand, and he readily sold his high-chief support to those who wished to sell anything to the naive natives. One of those items was liquor of one sort or another. Partnerships in several of the ramshackle saloons provided him the essential money to 'trade' and a cheap source of liquor. And the animosity of the missionaries.

He had readily adopted foreign clothing, particularly the military costumes offered him as an ali'i. They were like many of the new things, attractive, gaudy, and uncomfortable. But useful at times ... to appear to conform, to show his own regal style, to show that a Kanaka could be as prideful as the arrogant newcomers.

He particularly liked the hats, an item which was completely new to the Kanaka.

Earlier in the day, after Byron had boarded his ship, Boki had immediately shucked his stifling uniform. But he kept the hat on. Its brim shaded his eyes, and the felt crown gave him an additional inch or so of height with which to confront the Queen—who stood at six feet two. When she chose to stand.

He waited before her clad only in the hat and the scanty malo—barely covering his privates.

"May I sit with you ... Majesty?" Lord Byron had called her that, and she had immediately insisted that it become a regular title. She glanced at the expectant boy, and he scurried to collect a stack of sitting mats. She nodded to her right, but there was too little space between her and a porch post. The boy hesitated until she looked down at the top step, then back at her visitor.

The mats were too wide for the narrow tread, but Boki managed to sit, stretching his frame along the run of the steps, his head noticeably lower than his hostess.

"They are all gone now," he said, unknowingly matching the Queen's thoughts just when his visit had interrupted them.

"You are not talking about the English—"

"No. They are fools and not to be concerned about."

"Not such fools, cousin. I think they bide their time. With an empire so wide—"

"No, Majesty, our fools are gone. It is time to make new decisions. We have less to fear from distant English than near Americans."

"But Boki," the Queen jibed. "The American whalers made you rich. You have more dollars than—"

"Are you blind woman?" Boki was on his feet, his back to the monarch. "Or do you play me like an uku?" he demanded turning back. "The whalers have taken their filthy smelling ships and gone back to Boston, or wherever they came from. The Americans you must fear are the long-necks, the missionaries who destroy our culture, our way of life, like a makahiki rain melts kapa."

"Do you fear that they will melt your kapa malo and expose your naked member in a sinfully Christian way?"

"I do not fear any exposure of my member. Meles and hulas are performed in celebrations of its size and conquests. It is not my member that should occupy your thoughts!"

"What, brave chief? Tell me what you think I have not thought of already?"

"Our opportunity," he paused, looked across the top of the fence at the royal compound where the Queen's grass house stood, then back to the foreign steps before him. "The most destructive of all, the Queen

Mother, is dead. She, the most sacred chieftess of our race, was the first to flirt with this Christian poison. She is no longer an obstruction."

"You said yourself that we had too many Queens." With a smile, she continued, "How could she be our most sacred chieftess when she worshiped the white man's god?"

"Ha! You shouted down the King when he said that. Do you still mock the boy that you raised to be King, just because he failed so terribly?"

"It makes no difference. He too is dead."

"And Kaumua'ili is no longer a nuisance." A flicker of anger crossed the royal face. "Oh. Did I touch your heart, Majesty? He was your old-age toy. He was young and still handsome, and your wrinkled nose twitched when he was kidnapped and brought here for trial."

The Queen was on her feet. It was not the first time she had to confront Boki.

He was a high chief and had the support of many who had fallen victim to the tirades of the missionaries. But it was his opposition to other aspects of her government that had brought him perilously close to treason on more than one occasion.

She opted for the political retort, ignoring the personal affront. "And do I get no credit for substituting a kidnapping for a war? Were you to make so much money on an invasion of Kaua'i? Have we not all prospered in the ten years without a war? Would you undo all that the Great King accomplished by ending war?"

But Boki would not let go of the Queen's foible. "Do you deny that the Christianity of the Chief of Kaua'i was not a factor in your decision to let the longnecks stay?"

"The King allowed them to stay!"

"Madam!" He yelled the hated missionary title. "Liholiho did nothing without your bidding. He was a drunken boy whom you spoiled, and he probably welcomed a death that provided an escape from your hovering."

The loud voices had stirred sleeping neighbors, and reserve royal bodyguards appeared in case the need arose.

The Queen sat down. The boy fanned the flies. The reserves retreated. Boki kicked the mats aside and sat on the bare step. His back was turned to her when he spoke.

"The King's fatal journey to secure the protection of the British resulted in promises, but no documents of commitment. Liholiho's brother, a boy of thirteen, is made King by this convenient death. You still enjoy all the power the Great King bestowed on you as Kuhina Nui. We are more vulnerable to a Great Power take-over with every foreign gunboat's arrival. My ugly trader friends report regularly of what is happening in the big world beyond."

"And their news is not new. Ever since Vancouver began his unfortunate advice to the Great King, we have been warned of losing our islands to some foreign bully."

"Daily, the peril worsens. The massive country of China—I have seen the things called maps—and our small stones in the ocean are as grains of sand compared to China's vastness. But for all its size, it is being sliced up by the Great Powers. Even the youthful America tags along hoping for scraps from the kill as those hunters ravish the world. And the Yankee warships stop here, pausing on their way to such bad behavior."

"And any day one may stop and not go on. That is your fear?"

Boki did not answer.

"Is this what you learned in England while your King and Queen ate and drank too much?"

"Do not take my wife's stories too seriously. I think she was jealous of the attention the Royals got."

"I think it is more than that. Why does she refuse to take off the English clothes?"

Boki frowned at this distraction, but it was an issue with him too. "She is too much taken with the fact that English noblewomen change clothes five times a day. Liliha's head is easily turned by such trappings."

"Yes, the royal corpses were barely at rest when she announced her first party of what she called the 'season.'"

"It is a time of year when it is too cold to congregate outside. It is somewhat like our makahiki—when the weather is bad."

"She drinks too much."

This time Boki did not rise. Staring straight ahead he said, "Madam, you listen to too much idle talk."

"How can you expect the support of the other chiefs if the two of you are always drunk?"

"How can you expect the support of any Kanaka when you bend to every demand of the longnecks? They destroy our leadership by telling any who will listen that it is based on devil worship. They attack our sacred images and warn that the devil occupies our holy places."

"And you believe in this devil?"

"No, but they do, and they are making our people believe."

"Then we will tell them to leave."

Boki half-turned to her. This was new. "And what if they refuse?"

"Then we will round them up and force them onto the next ship that stops."

"As we did with the Catholic priests?"

"Yes."

"But there were only two of them. There are almost forty of these here already and more to arrive, or so I'm told."

"Yes, Reverend Bingham says there are plans to send a total of twelve boatloads."

"My god, woman! Do you see what you have caused? It may be too late. Liholiho made the people destroy our sacred images and their places."

"No. He told them to, but as usual, no one paid him any attention. I think the images have been hidden in the flooded kalo fields."

Boki was not mollified. His knowledge of the world had been greatly expanded by his visit to London, and there was a lot of new information that he was busily processing. Much of it was too sophisticated to be easily understood by his ignorant Queen and her Council.

"There is more in this twin threat. My English friends say that there is a great change happening in the world. All countries are looking for something that is cheap and can be changed into something costly to sell."

"And how is that a threat to us?"

"Our ignorance. My ugly trader friends tell me that what they call sugar cane grows wild in our fields. It requires no attention. When its stalks are mashed, and the juice boiled it becomes a powder, a trade good so expensive that only the rich can afford it."

"So, we will chop it down and sell it to the haoles."

"No. There is not enough to make it worthwhile. It must be done as we grow sweet potatoes—in large fields that cover entire mountainsides and valleys. Already a foreigner pays a chief of Kaua'i to use several valleys for growing fruit on trees. He sells the fruit to every ship captain to prevent his crew's disease." He turned now to face the Queen. "Many chiefs will want to get money from idle lands that their people do not farm. It is called 'renting' the land."

"Only chiefs have these ahupua'a, and we can prohibit them from this 'renting.'

"Perhaps, but there is gossip that a young bachelor missionary has fallen in love with the daughter of a chief and she has promised him vast amounts of land on Kaua'i if they marry. No renting necessary."

"Bingham will not allow a rebellion such as that."

"There are others. Olohana's bride brought large tracts along with her skinny okole to his bed. The Scotsman, Cleghorn, makes hang-dog smiles at Paki's youngest. He is promised several valleys if Paki approves the match."

"Boki, you are a dangerous man. I have thought about killing you. The missionaries would silently approve. There are other chiefs who are jealous of your position and your wealth, and they too would welcome your disappearance. There is only one thing preventing me from having you sacrificed. It is your drunken associates from whom only you can find out what is happening in the bigger world."

"No, you can no longer sacrifice me, because the longnecks would never allow it, even though they'd like to see me gone. But there is a big world beyond, and I've become very aware of it and constantly learn of what is going on there. We cannot know too much about that world and its happenings. You need me. The Kingdom needs me."

"Call the Council of Chiefs. We will meet at the birth of the new moon and find new directions before it wanes. Any more time will be idle argument. You must report all that happened in London before the Royals died. You must tell us what your drunken trader friends know of this 'buy cheap, sell high.'"

Boki stood to leave. The Queen dismissed him with a wave, and he turned toward the gate. As he walked away, she studied this huge handsome man in the prime of his life. She knew of those mele and hula that celebrated his sexual prowess, and she wondered about taking him to her bed—just as a precaution. As she had done with the kidnapped Chief of Kaua'i.

But then, there was a lot of gossip about that, and it had probably been part of what riled his son to rebellion. There were plenty of other young men to dally with. No need to stir up political hu-hu when so much fresh meat abounded with no strings attached.

A New Moon

Kuakini, the Queen's brother and governor of Hawai'i Island sat down after a passionate defense of the charge against him of misusing the 'governments money.'

He had charged his accusers to define this term, 'government,' which he called a missionary word and not usable in dealing with Kanaka issues.

There was a mumble of serious exchanges from the rows of chiefs who sat before the Queen on mats spread on the grass. A breeze blew down from the Ko'olaus across Manoa Valley. The meeting was held there in the hopes that the comfort of the surroundings would support clear thinking, patience, and cooperation.

Ka'ahumanu explained again this difficult new concept that separated a part of the tax, that traditionally was wholly the property of the ruling chiefs, into private and public shares.

Boki sat in the front row, I was in the same row, but at the opposite end. He was very much to the side, struggling to cope with his boredom and his impatience with the ignorance of this council which was growing less and less capable of dealing with the world that encroached upon it—with every ship that stopped. It was this ineptitude that prompted the struggle he had with the missionary pressure to form legislative bodies and cabinets and other foreign governmental entities. He was sure they would become instruments to befuddle and take advantage of the Kanaka.

Finally, Ka'ahumanu stopped the prattle and introduced Boki. She had laid particular emphasis on his report of the London visit, so he dutifully recounted that sad tale amid many pitiful wails of 'aue!'

To the one or two more akama'i than the rest, the passing of the young King would be an improvement in the quality of leadership. They were as impatient as Boki to get to the planning that would now be required. Because of that, there was some grumbling when Boki urged his companion to stand.

The youth displayed his Caucasus roots by the shock of blond hair and blue eyes. His beard had been carefully trimmed that morning, on Boki's orders, in an attempt to make this haole as presentable as possible to such an august body as the Council of Chiefs of the Kingdom of Hawai'i.

His worn Russian naval uniform, even with its random crease or two did little to aid him in the eyes of many in the audience who often wore the gaudiest of western military regalia.

When it was revealed that he was a deserter from a Russian research vessel, nine years earlier, the Queen's interest quickened. The captain of that ship, Otto Von Kotzebue, had visited her and had permitted her to fondle his curly hair.

The chiefs remembered that King Kamehameha had been far less friendly when informed of the Captain's mission. The Great King and his Council had been shaken to the core. The visit was part of the ongoing effort to make a deal between the Czarist government and Hawai'i that would effectively surrender the Kingdom to foreign rule.

I had warned the King and council at that time of the Russian Bear's European adventures. We had already rejected the overtures of the Russian agent, Dr. Scheffer, and sent him packing. But he had gone no further than Kaua'i and had been Kaumua'ili's treacherous downfall.

That sorry Chief's name produced a ruffle of muttering when it was spoken.

"Listen!" Boki hushed them in an effort to keep their attention focused, then he carefully translated the next portion of the youth's recitation.

"The great Czar of Russia has expanded his fleet of ships in the Northern Pacific Ocean, and our land claims stretch south into Spanish California. As our colonies north of Japan and along the west coast of North America expand and export their rich commodities to China and the East, they will require the support of many resupply ports along the way."

It was the same argument that I had thwarted before. When I had the King's ear.

A buzz of conversation rattled among the chiefs, but Boki hushed them.

"In return for your cooperation in such an arrangement, the Czar is prepared to make all your people citizens of the greatest empire in the world. The Russian army will protect your islands from any European King hungry for new conquests, and your citizens will become Orthodox Christians, true Christians, protected from the marauding Protestant heretics."

It was necessary again for Boki's chiding; then he nodded to the youth to go on.

"Just as we have done in our dealings with native peoples in the North, you may continue to follow your tribal ways with protections of all your religious teachings."

"It is a little late for that!" someone grumbled aloud, inciting a general uproar.

Liholiho's lifting of the kapu, effectively destroying the Kanaka religion and the Chiefs' basis on which to justify their rule, had left many ruffled feathers. They all knew that the young King did nothing without the permission or urging of Ka'ahumanu.

She was immediately on her feet. As usual, her simple turn toward them was enough to quiet their clamor. "Ah, we have another opportunity to become 'true' Christians. This will be the fourth, counting the nervous efforts of the Anglicans—who are afraid of competing with the fiery American Calvinists."

The ensuing silence ratified the fact that the religious issues were far too complex for the unsophisticated chiefs to comprehend and they were perfectly willing to have Boki and the Queen deal with those who came to threaten them with an everlasting roast in their own earthen ovens.

She turned on the visitor, who took a step back. "Olohana tells us that you kill many furry animals in the North and sell their pelts to the Chinese." The lad glanced at me, then nodded as Boki translated.

The Queen appeared not to hear and continued her train of thought. "And your merchants will become very wealthy because their ships can stop here for supplies and repairs. What will you do to make my people wealthy? Boki already sells the white man's firewater. And our valleys are stripped of sandalwood to pay for huge beds too hot to sleep in ... so we have little to sell."

Boki answered, "Olohana has taught us to make each ship that comes to our harbor pay. But many are too large to cross the reef. The Czar's men will make it possible for all ships to enter."

The Queen turned to me. "Then they all will pay?"

Boki answered, "Yes. And they will pay to use the old whaler's warehouses and buy repair parts for hull and rigging."

"From your drunken friends," I added.

The Queen paced as she pondered the information. Boki did not let her think so long that she might arrive at an argument against the plan. "Francisco de la Marin and I, along with other chiefs, are planting our valleys with food for these ships. Paniolos are catching the wild cows, and we will salt the beef to keep it from spoiling. Ship captains will pay well for food that has not been in barrels for many years."

"So, if we are to eat, we must depend on providing the needs of those who come from away?"

"No, we can still grow food for our people. Not all valleys will be used for foreign food."

"Then what need have we for these new preachers of sin? If we can feed ourselves, then we can live without them. For countless generations, we lived here without the aid of the outsiders. Our population is much smaller now because of the diseases they bring, so surely we can again do without them."

There was a general grumble among the seated chiefs.

"Aue! Do you so need the bed with four posts to believe that you are ali'i? Do you need Boki's firewater to excuse your bad behavior?" She paused and turned to Boki and the youth. "The only thing you bring is protection from some other grasping thief."

She let the ripple of conversation go on for a time. Boki sat with his head down.

The decision had already been made. Everyone knew it, but this drama must be played out.

"If I say no?"

Boki jumped to his feet. "The Russians are teetering on losing all their Pacific possessions. Their small colonies on the North American coast have never been self-supporting. Their constant European adventures demand resources that drain the Czar's treasury."

Two chiefs, from among Ka'ahumanu's favorites, stood up. With a slight motion of her head, she signaled that they should sit again. "Don't you mean 'wars' when you say adventures?" She looked searchingly at Boki. "And rebellions."

A small boy who had been fanning the Queen earlier suddenly stood up, and I handed him a San Francisco newspaper. He proudly read the headline, "Russians Win Turk War Amid Unrest at Home." He smiled broadly.

The Queen patted the boy's head. "He goes to the longneck's school every day," she paused, "Will he have to go to the Russian's school now?"

"All Russian citizens speak and read Russian," the sailor said proudly.

"Olohana says that most of your citizens are ignorant peasants who cannot write their name." She looked at me for confirmation.

But Boki was tired of the game. "If you say no—"

"If I say no it is because the devil I know is better than the devil I don't know."

"Olohana again!"

The Queen looked at me, and I stood, head bowed.

"I have not listened to him as the old King did, but sometimes the things he has to say make more sense than you or the missionaries, or ..." she paused, resting her gaze on the rumpled Russian, "new saviors." She turned toward the group and as if by some signal, they rose facing her. "I am tired of being saved by those who profit daily by their mere presence here. I say no."

It was not the final nail in the coffin of the Russian Pacific Fleet. That would come at the battle with Japan at Port Arthur in Manchuria, where the entire fleet would be sunk. By depriving the Russians of a year-round ice-free port—something they had to fight two more wars while seeking—their North American posts failed, and they had no Pacific base to build upon.

The Hawaiian Kingdom never felt free of the constant outside threat. As late as the 1840s, Hawaiian delegations pleaded for independent recognition in all the world's capitols.

However, the real threat had always been an internal one. By then the sons of the missionaries had returned from New England Universities at the peak of the Industrial Revolution. Amid the constant pressure to mimic a democracy, the Island government was regularly biased in favor of their commercial interests. By the end of the century, they overthrew the Monarchy and traded the Islands to the United States in exchange for duty-free entry of their sugar.

Had Ka'ahumanu said no to the missionaries in 1821, perhaps she could have saved the Kingdom from the United States, but there were other regular threats.

Had she said yes to the Russians, then Japan would have attacked Pearl Harbor against an old enemy instead of a new one.

La Cercle de la Vie

Kendall Bartels

We were poor, desperately poor. Poor enough that one of maman's many male visitors had called us destitute rats—something that bothered me enough to remind my sister of it years after it had been said to us, years after we had escaped that grimy little room and the hunger and the brutal sounds of skin slapping skin. Marie had not remembered the comment, but tossed her head back and coughed her bark of a laugh between drawls from her cigarette, she did not doubt that it had been said.

"There were so many men ... perhaps, it is a family habit to surround yourself with men for—what did maman say, Catherine, it was for protection?" Marie said, staring at me with dark eyes that dared me to protest her implication. Her greasy hair and dirt-smudged face were an embarrassment to me in the café I visited regularly. I had invited her out of the need to see her, had thought light of filling her stomach with bread and sending her on her way, had not realized how out of place she would be on this side of Paris, only a few streets away from the opera house.

"We were fortunate." I spoke as I sipped black coffee, tilting my nose away from her smoke and out toward the gleaming window facing the streets of Paris, "It was one of her visitors who has supported us all these years."

It was a yellow day, hot enough that I had dreaded tugging on stockings after changing out of my ballet tights, and yet breezy enough that my fan could remain collapsed on the table between Marie and me. I feared if I opened it and she saw the silk muscles between the boning that she would grow crueler. I had dressed in the simplest clothes that I could manage to wear outside, a petticoat made of azure silk, with my smallest bustle. Still, Marie persisted.

"Supported you, you mean." It was odd to see my sneer reflected back to me on someone else's face, peculiar to see my hair dirty in front of me even though I had bathed that morning, shocking to see my skin tanned and dirt under my nails.

"If Monsieur Chaufourier had not offered me a position in the ballet I would have no money to send to you. So yes, he has supported us both."

Silence slipped between us, Marie no doubt resenting that I mentioned that I sent her money and me tired of having to defend the way I survived and supported us both. Marie had always had the horrible habit of trying to guilt me for surviving, for doing exactly what she would have done had she been in my position. The bell tinkled, and we both turned expectantly toward the door.

I straightened at the sight of the girls I knew from work bustling into the café, their hair piled high in buns which mirrored my own, smiles frozen on their lips at the sight of my mirror image and I sitting together. There would be no mistaking our relation as the three girls came nearer, curious of the sister I had never mentioned.

"Bonjour Catherine!" Patricia, Meg, and Celeste greeted me in harmonious chimes after waving to the boy behind the counter, their regular orders of black coffee being started for them before they wandered to our little table in the corner.

Marie raised her eyebrows at their coquettish voices, smug amusement written across her features as I felt a prickly blush inch across my collarbone, up my neck. I was ashamed of my past and of my present meeting, and both were suddenly aware that I worked to hide each from the other.

I echoed their greetings before Meg asked in her thick English accent, "Catherine, is this your sister?"

"Oui, Marie let me introduce to you mademoiselles Meg, Patricia, and Celeste." They nodded in her direction as she stared them down, dark eyebrows unmoving and chapped lips unsmiling as she crossed her arms.

"Bonjour." My sister's voice was flat, gruff, so low compared to my sing-song that I had not realized I affected around my peers.

There was an angry burn mark in the shape of the butt end of a cigar on her forearm that I had not noticed before. I saw Celeste's brown eyes spot the scar, a look of understanding passing over her face. I knew that the whole company would know by the time the week was out—they would hear of my dirty sister, the manmade injury on her arm, my past which must be sordid if I worked so hard to conceal it for the entirety of the seven years I had been with the company.

"We dance together," I supplied to the stagnant conversation, ashamed at my relation's rudeness, flailing for purchase as I gave her a pointed look that she could not ignore.

"How fortunate you all are, to be able to spend so much time with my sister," Marie decided.

"Yes, we are all so very fond of her," Patricia complimented, leaving me to politely admit that it was I who was the lucky one to be surrounded by their talent.

"And did Monsieur Chaufourier collect you, as well?" Marie challenged, chin rising and purposeful gaze dragging along their bodies, turn by turn.

"Marie!" I was scandalized, there were no words for the humiliation she had caused. How she had berated me, for months before in her letters, for never inviting her to my corner of the world. For only visiting her flat on weekends when I was sure the rest of the company would be away and unable to know where I had gone. How awfully she repaid me for finally extending an invitation, for giving up one of my scarce breaks from rehearsal to be berated by the only family I had left.

"Meg, Patricia, Celeste—I cannot apologize enough, my sister is—"

"Unwell, clearly." Celeste decided, pity curtaining in her eyes as she stepped away, Meg and Patricia eager to follow and remove themselves from Marie's unabashed gaze.

"Yes, clearly. Catherine, we will see you in rehearsal tomorrow?" Meg asked, her French heavy and swollen in her mouth, not waiting for my response as the trio turned away to silently seek the table outside, out of sight from my spot near the window.

"Marie! How could you?" My hiss was low enough that the boy behind the counter could not hear, though I was sure the way I leaned across the table with tears blurring my vision was hint enough of what had transpired between the beautiful, familiar dancers and the dirty woman who sat across from me. "You know how hard I have tried to hide this part of my life, of how hard I work to better myself for the benefit of all of us, and yet you come here and—"

"Answer me this, Catherine, does Monsieur Chaufourier continue to find positions for you? It would seem that he does.

Your friends' dresses are not as fine as yours is, their ears are naked where you wear diamonds."

Only my sisterly affection for her kept me from standing and bustling away. Only the fact that she had scrambled to inhale both her and my slivers of baguette kept me from swearing that I would never see her again. Only guilt that it had been me who Monsieur Chaufourier had favored, and not my sister who was only eleven months my junior—my equal in all ways but kindness—kept me from abandoning her to go sit with my fellow ballerinas and tearfully admit a fabrication about my mad, widowed sister.

I blinked away my tears, watching as the boy began to fill a tray with a pot and cups, balanced it on his hand before he exited the café with the little bell tinkling behind him.

Incapable of leaving, I stared at Marie. My single sister who took the money that I sent her and spilled it away on drinks, my dark sister who could not hold a job for the liquor on her breath, my sad sister who had been in love once but had had an operation to remove a baby that had been unwanted by the father.

"Nonsense," I sniffed, "my dress is outdated, no matter the quality of the silk. They choose to wear poorer versions of the most recent fashion, that is all."

"They do not wear diamonds in their ears, or any other jewelry."

"We have all just changed after morning rehearsal, perhaps they do not wear earrings on their break for fear of forgetting to remove them before our day resumes."

"I find that unlikely. Tell me, Catherine, where did you get your earrings?"

I finished my coffee and set the empty cup back in its saucer, choosing to focus on the watery blue print of the porcelain rather than meet Marie's shrewd scrutiny.

"I acquire my jewelry in the same way as many ballerinas at the opera, through gracious patrons and appreciators of our art."

"Art, yes," Marie smiled before slurping the rest of her coffee, letting her cup clatter into its saucer before she continued, "And yet they were all so happy to see your shame, so curious to know why you would sit with a destitute rat."

I had not considered that she would think that I still thought of her in that way. It hurt to be incapable of denying that I was mortified by her. How nice it must be for sisters who are able to tell each other that they love each other, with no shame or pain or jealousy or guilt, I wondered if such sisters existed.

"You would not be so insufferable if you knew of my predicament."

"Then why don't you tell me, Catherine? Did you think that I would be shocked to hear that you needed something from me? Did you think that I would accept this sudden change without question, surely even you must realize, that finally allowing me to visit you is suspicious? It would be only for your benefit that you bring me here, there is nothing for me at your opera house—this I learned long ago." Blame laced her words, spite danced in her eyes.

"Marie if you will not be kind then I cannot tell you," I warned.

"No, if you expected me to be kind, you would not have invited me."

At want for something to do, I picked up the pot between us and poured us fresh cups of coffee. Skin suddenly cold even after touching the warm container, my hands shook as I carefully set the glass top of the sugar bowl to the side and used silver tongs to drop three cubes of sugar into her cup, one into mine. The conversant sound of the delicate glass of the sugar bowl's top sliding against the glass of the sugar bowl itself comforted me in its familiarity.

Marie waited until I sat back in my seat, eyes traversing up the wrinkled floral pattern of her petticoat and worn grey Caraco jacket that I had retired to her. If she had not made me feel so dirty for living so well, I might have invited her back to my home, to take whichever clothes of mine that she liked. But I could not do so, I knew that any gifts would be received with unkindness and that she would question why I was so ready to give away clothes. I would have to face the acknowledgment that Monsieur Chaufourier would gladly replace whatever Marie took.

"Come, come Catherine. What is it that you need me to fix for you?" Marie spoke as if she had never solved any problems in her life besides the question of where her next drink would come from.

"Do you remember," and then I was forced to pause as the bell tinkled and the boy reappeared, metal tray relaxed at his side as he sent us a smile before returning to the secluded backroom. Only once we had privacy did I try again while leaning forward, voice lowered in the noiseless café, "do you remember the situation you found yourself in three years ago? With Jacques Girardot?"

If I had thought Marie's eyes had been guarded before, they became a fortress with the mention of his name. What little light had been left in her was distinguished, her tan ran pale, if it were possible for her hair to have flattened at the sound of a name, then it would have done.

"Catherine, do not tell me you are in the way that I was."

I looked away, out to the streets of Paris once more. The cobblestones were clean from the previous evening's rain, giving the deceiving appearance that the city and its people were well looked after, well cared for—if a tourist were to visit they could only think the highest of how France looked after its own.

In the silence of the café, with only my sister close enough to bear witness to my defeat, I spoke my truth aloud for the first time in the two months that I had known of it, "I'm with child."

"Oh Catherine, tell me you aren't." Crystalline tears wetted her eyelashes and shame filled me once more, inflated my stomach, pushed upwards toward my lungs which suddenly felt so exposed.

"I need the name," and Marie gasped at my words, not needing me to finish my request to know what I was asking, "of the woman who assisted you."

"Catherine, you do not want that." Her bony wrist hitting the table through her stained glove, sending the tongs clattering, the lid of the sugar bowl dancing in its seat, my spoon rattling against the saucer. She touched me for the first time that day, grasping my fingers in her own and squeezing hard, not allowing me to escape the tense pain in her eyes as she repeated herself, "Trust me, you do not want that."

"No, I do not." The bell tinkled as I spoke, "But I must."

The bell chimed as a young couple entered the space—him in a fine suit and sophisticated spectacles, her in a lavender dress and blonde hair piled high above a lightly powdered face—with a small boy in a blue suit hanging off their hands between them. The man carried a pair of shining gloves in his free hand, and the woman had a gold band set with a large diamond on her ring finger. She was all that I was not, all that I could never be, and seemed to have everything I ever dreamed of having. As the serving boy reappeared from the back room to take the family's orders, I wondered if the way I felt about this blonde was the way Marie felt about me. I assumed it was so.

After the family had established themselves at the table next to our own and fell into a conversation, I asked my sister to write down the name and address of the woman who had helped her.

"You do not want to be found having her name. You'll have to remember it."

I nodded in agreement, my body feeling as if it belonged entirely to someone else as I leaned forward to hear the name and address.

Madame Lublanc. Farther from the opera house than even Marie lived. I could already imagine the filth that surrounded her, wondered what I would wear to visit her— knew that I could not go dressed in finery, could not risk drawing enough attention to have someone ask me my name. What would happen once I was inside was too horrible to consider, to even attempt to imagine, I could not contemplate how I would make myself go through with it. Moreover, I was afraid.

"Do you have someone to go with you? You will need help getting home."

"I'll hire a coach."

"They'll know what you are doing. Let me go with you. Spend the night with me. He knows I exist, at least. Not even he could deny you one night to yourself after seven years."

I realized then that Marie blamed Monsieur Chaufourier for this, that she believed this to be another act of cruelty that he was demonstrating. As if saving me from my forsaken childhood had been an act of cruelty, as if he had ever shown me an act of outright unkindness, as if I had not been a willing participant in my life for the past seven years. My stomach turned at the thought of returning to him the day after it was finished, of having to find a lie to cover what bodily damage was done to me or explain why I could not stop crying.

"You look ill."

A rousing echo of laughs from the family beside us burst through the café.

"I am ill."

"Yes, I suppose you are."

Silent grief swallowed us and the vague wonder of why my mother had failed to go through with the surgery twice swam behind my mind. Perhaps, the bitter thought soiled my thoughts even further, she could not afford it.

When we left the café, I bought us a cup of raspberries to share as we walked, her gritty fingers crinkling the paper cup as she scooped four or five pieces of fruit into her mouth all at once. Marie was always hungry. My hunger came to me in one swoop of exhaustion from a long rehearsal, right before I fell asleep in a warm bed, with either Monsieur Chaufourier's warm arm heavy against my abdomen or my wet hair fanned out all around me after a long bath. I could not survive hunger the way that Marie did, could not imagine returning to days at a time where no food was to be had. I had no ballerina sister to send me money for me to waste on drink instead of food. The ink of the raspberries stained the fingers of her gloves pink, nearly red; I had a dress that exact color in my closet that Monsieur Chaufourier liked for me to wear to the parties thrown after opening nights at the opera. He said it made my skin glow.

Marie scrambled for more fruit, too impulsive to be shy in her actions. The sun was beginning to slip from its reign of noon, sliding down and casting shadows as it was taken ransom by clouds and the tall Parisian buildings. Her arm on mine felt heavy, as finite as sunlight. Church bells rang, our evening rehearsal would begin in an hour, I was thankful that I would not need to return home to fetch new clothes, my costume was already waiting for me backstage. A breeze slipped through the skinny alleyways as we approached the opera house, brushed across my cheeks, rustled my petticoat.

"Tomorrow." I decided as Marie finished the last berry.

"Tomorrow." My sister agreed.

I had never had to keep anything from Monsieur Andre Chaufourier before. With him knowing my past, assisting my present, and promising my future, it so happened that he was the only person in my life who knew all sides of me. Hiding my past or my sister would have been useless, he had experienced our mother's depravity himself. He knew all of my present, as a main director of the ballet, he often had control over my routine; my future was in the promises dangling from his fingers in magnificent gifts of sparkling ruby necklaces and lush velvet-lined cloaks and muffs of mink.

"You're quiet tonight," he murmured, his pointed chin resting on my shoulder as I observed myself dabbing rose water along my neck, where he had asked me to dab it when I was fifteen years old, where he liked to lean forward and inhale against my skin.

"Am I?" In the dark apartment with candlelight pouring into the mirror of my vanity, we made quite the pair. Andre was all greying hair, long jaw, permanently pale cheeks, with thin lips, and creases around his eyes and between his salt and pepper eyebrows. The pallor of his face and grey in his hair brought amber hues to my brown roots below my bun, roses to my cheeks, raspberries to my lips.

"Very quiet." Andre smiled at me, the usual affection there. Candlelight painted us gold and sparked a fire in Andre's eyes as he pressed a damp kiss to my cheekbone, his closeness bringing me his scent of tobacco and cognac. Large, bony hands rested on my shoulders, warm through the periwinkle silk of my night robe, and gave me a kindly squeeze.

"I thought of you often today. I missed your darling little self, rummaging around backstage ... How was your sister?"

Dirty, poor, hungry, relying on me—but those were constant, obvious. I couldn't say that. He did not keep me in this beautiful flat, surrounded by beautiful things, dressed in expensive clothes to hear me whine. If he had any inclination to hear a woman's worries he might have spent the night with his wife.

"Good, darling, thank you for asking."

"Did you miss me too?" Andre asked, our eyes locked in the glass and his face looking all the longer next to my short, round one. When he was needy like this, I knew that I would have to bargain to get what I liked.

"Of course, my love."

At this he crooked a long finger beneath my chin and tilted my lips toward his, claiming a lingering kiss before he turned away to his changing station where he began unwinding his cravat.

"I was thinking," my voice was too casual to my own ears, but he did not seem to notice, "it might be nice for me to see her again tomorrow, she's invited me to spend the night with her, but I would have to miss evening rehearsal ..."

Through the mirror I could see my words stop the flow of his movements, he straightened and turned to me, the eyes of our reflections met.

"Are you asking me or telling me?" He said, returning to his task of undressing but with his eyes still focused on me.

Trying not to appear concerned, I was scared of him denying me something simply because I asked for it, knowing his habit of enjoying denial for the sense of delayed satisfaction when he would later gift me my previously voiced desires as a surprise. I began removing my pins from my bun, and let my dark locks unravel and flow to rest around my waist.

Seeing a glint of admiration, of want, of need in him, I decided to test my luck, push his boundaries, keep him young, like he asked me to but only responded well to on days that business had gone his way.

"I'm telling you."

"You know, of course, that I will expect something in return?" A coy smirk played across his lips, bringing youth to his face and light to his eyes as he shrugged out of and hanged his jacket.

I lifted my chin at the challenge.

"What if I say no?" His eyebrows rose at my tone, of the solidity there, of my flattened spine and set shoulders.

"What if you say no?" Andre mused, rolling his shirtsleeves up to reveal veiny arms and knobby wrists. I watched, stock still as he strode toward me, the same knowing smile scribed in his features as he grew closer. Large hands set themselves on my shoulders once more, this time light as he gently nudged me from my seated position and turned me to face him.

Towering with at least a head or two of height on me, Andre stood close enough that I had to tilt my chin up to meet his eyes. Then he stroked my cheeks with the back of his fingers, ran his hands along the waves of my hair, and brushed his knuckles across my silk-covered breasts, before tucking his fingers into the sash of my robe so that he held me by my leash.

A shivery sigh fell through me, the kind he liked to hear, and a shallow moan was unfolded from the depths of his chest. The knot sat in the space between his hands, untouched and momentarily retaining my modesty. My gaze followed his thumb stroking the knot, his voice lifted my eyes back to find his whitish lips.

"Don't you want to make me happy, Catherine?" *I want to have a place to live.* "Don't you want to make me proud?" *I want my sister to have food to eat.*

My response should have been immediate, grateful, awed. I took too long to answer, stood in silence for too long, he tugged on the knot so that our ankles collided. 'Adore me,' said his eyes. One hand abandoned my sash, moved up and cupped at the damp back of my neck, to cradle me tighter against him.

"Don't you want me?"

"Of course, I do," I placated, my smile coming easy once I pushed his hand away from the knot of my robe and pulled the sash free on my own. The sash slithered to the floor and the robe opened, my bare body exposed to his hungry eyes; the heat of his hands as he grasped my naked waist drove a shudder through me. I did not feel whole in his arms, did not want to think of his baby pressed fragile and vulnerable inside me, did not feel present under his studious gaze.

A flicker of doubt passed through his eyes, but he must have written my shudder off as one of pleasure.

I nursed him into goodwill as I pressed myself against his clothed body in a tight hug, so that his arms joined my body beneath my robe, "How could you even ask if I want you?" I murmured the sensation of hearing my words but not having been the one to speak them making me dizzy, thankful for his long arms around my waist to steady me.

"Will I be rewarded for giving you what you want?" He asked, one hand sliding down to smooth over the curve of my bottom and the other reaching up to stroke my hair as I kept my face hidden against the buttons of his shirt.

"Yes," I spoke as I looked up at him, eyes blinking but body steady.

"Show me." I took a step back, away from him, and purposefully rolled my shoulders. The robe slipped away from my skin, leaving me bare; I took his hand and led him to bed.

Madame Lublanc was not as old as I would have wished for her to be. She seemed to be only ten years older than I was; she was haggard, with wiry red hair that corkscrewed out of her scalp and rested around her fat, freckled arms.

After my morning rehearsal, I had walked to Marie's house, silent and shivering though the day was beautiful and sunlight poured through the streets of Paris as if clouds had never existed before.

Celeste had invited me to join her and the others for coffee, but I had declined. Instead, I walked, terror making me deaf to the world before I let Marie shove me out of my clothes and then into her own. A brown cloak, tattered around the bottom and ripped on one of the shoulders, had been tied around my neck and hooded around my head.

If I had been asked for directions back to Marie's I would not have been able to give them, I saw, heard, and thought nothing. The alleys were dark, rodent infested, and stunk of piss and death—but I did not notice. Guiding me all the way, gripping my arm and practically shoving me up the steps to the small nook of an establishment, Marie was beside me from her house to the rickety bench in the foyer of Lublanc's business.

There was a grey curtain shielding the window of the door, keeping light from the streets out and trapping us within. Marie's hand was clammy in my own, her fingers tight around my numb ones. I had never asked my sister about her experience in that dark part of town, and as I sat, legs trembling and heart gagging me with its incessant pounding in my throat, I was glad that Marie had not told me what to expect.

There were two doors, one that Lublanc had disappeared behind after briefly greeting us at the door, and the other that a girl, around the age of eleven, had scurried out of when Lublanc loudly complained about having to open the door herself.

Some clanging, metal on metal, and then the clunking of wood on wood, sounded from Lublanc's door, the far one. Marie and I sat together, statues, years of grief and resentment and pain buried between us beneath our need, our fear, and our pain.

"Is this what you want?" Marie asked.

"What if I say no?" I whispered to her, with the weight of a life of misery pressing on me, haunting me.

"Then you cannot do this. You'll think about this moment every day for the rest of your life, either way." Her hisses filled the space, rattled my mind with their urgency, "Catherine, is this truly what you want?"

"Yes." I lied, and then added, "I cannot give up my life, cannot give up the money."

Then the young girl appeared, blonde hair tied away from her face as she called out the fake name I had given.

"Triste?"

"Oui."

Marie had to pry me from her grasp and help me to my feet, my birth name a whisper as she encouraged me to go forward.

I could barely see for the white sheet of panic and fear numbing my eyes, wiping logic away. The young girl spoke to me, but I could not hear her as I was led into Lublanc's room. It was dark, the window covered, a fire burning in the grate, a wooden table was the centerpiece of the room, a leather bag looked worn on an end table, a collection of canes in the corner, there was also a stained couch. I could feel cold sweat pricking my neck.

It was hot. The fire burned my cheeks, the blonde girl's sweat dampened her cotton blouse, red wires clung to Lublanc's forehead. Lublanc leaned on the table, no pity nor judgment in her eyes, she did this every day.

There were hundreds of women in Paris grateful for her services, hundreds of girls who kept their lives because they did not give birth to another, hundreds of women who took control and made a decision.

Lublanc spoke low, soothing, soft, and slow—giving the impression that she knew not to startle me, was afraid to spook me away. It was meant to comfort me, but her acknowledging my fear confirmed that I had the right to be afraid. She instructed me to take off my underclothes, I could keep my skirts on. If I wanted to hold them up around my waist, I could, if I wanted to keep them on

I could but I would need to wear something else home.

I turned my back, barely registering the young girl's swooping motions as a piece of material was laid over the wood table, and shyly pulled off my underclothes and underskirts. The girl's hands were small and warm in mine as she helped me step up onto the table. I laid back, indecent, holding my skirts up around my waist. Suddenly, I was grateful that the fire remained burning. The blonde flitted around the room, I stared at the dark flatness of the ceiling; I listened as candles were lit, a chair was dragged close to my dangling legs, the leather bag was opened, metal clinked together.

A hand rested on my knee, spread my legs further. Tears blurred my vision until the ceiling was a black blur floating above me.

"Ines will press on your stomach; in a little while, she will give you a stick to bite."

I had not realized I was sobbing until Lublanc spoke and had to raise her voice from its once lilting tones to be heard over my undignified crying. I could not see them.

When Ines put her hands on my bare stomach, resting just below my belly button at the place that I was sure would begin to swell in just a few weeks more, I startled.

Lublanc, grabbing my swinging ankle, asked me if I would like her to tether my leg to the leg of the table. My control was slipping with every second, my shoulders arched into the hardwood beneath me, my heart clattered, my pulse rushed, dizziness was beaten out by nausea.

"Catherine?" The blonde did not bother with my fake name as she kept one hand on my naked stomach and placed the other on my dripping cheek.

"Are you ready?" A little pressure fell on me, made me squirm, and I screamed.

I could not do it. Their faces were surprised—the realization that my display up to that point had not been inordinate, had been expected, shook me further—and I pushed the blonde away as I gasped for air, my vision prickling and focusing as I shoved my skirts down to cover myself and fought myself off the table.

The woman and the girl stood back, watched as I struggled with my shaking fingers to yank my clothes back onto my swaying body. The heat from the fire scolded me, I could feel their eyes on each strand of my hair, nausea swirled up through me once more, and I gagged on the air and my tears.

"We cannot give you your money back, mademoiselle." The blonde contritely informed me, as if she would change my mind.

Marie's eyes were wide when she saw me, and tears slipped from her eyes when she saw my clean skirts and able body. I tried to walk past her to the door, I tried to flee from the entire situation and return home to Monsieur Andre's needy arms and warm bed.

Tomorrow, I decided as my sister caught me by my arms and pulled me into a hug as I wetly sobbed into the crook of her neck. Tomorrow I would wake up and take a long bath in Andre's spacious tub, and then I would tell him that I love him, and he would leave his wife, and we would marry. And I would no longer have to rehearse for nine hours a day nor I would I have to worry how an unwed mother would continue to dance for such little pay.

"Catherine, you said—"

"I cannot do it, Marie!" Her hands petted my hair as I shook, my eyes were squeezed closed against my tears, but still, they streamed down to wet my cheeks, my neck, my collarbone, my blouse.

"Shh, Catherine, it is alright. You do not have to, you do not have to ..." Rocking me the way our mother had when we were little, Marie let me cry against her until my moans resided into shameful hiccups as the truth poured over me. I was not as strong as Marie, I could not handle pulling out this baby that I already loved.

"How did you do it?" I begged against her skin, smelling filth and sweat and love on her.

"I am not as brave as you," Marie said, smoothing hands comforting me as we rocked side to side, "I cannot love like you can."

Another strangled sob, dry save for my sniveling, wracked my body and tore at my throat. "What do I do, Marie? What do I do?"

Seven months before Adette was born, I was removed from the Paris Opera Ballet. I was allowed to take my clothes from the flat Monsieur Andre had put me up in. The jewelry was gone before I had the chance to ask to keep the diamond earrings that Monsieur Andre had given to me on my first birthday with him, when I still had the brightness of youth in my eyes and hope for the future in my heart. I had thought that I would like to be able to gift the earrings to Adette one day, perhaps she would be the first woman in our family to marry, and could wear them then.

Monsieur Andre kissed me goodbye without apologizing for making me go but saying that he would miss me.

I did not beg, I did not make a show of it. My belly was too round for my tutu to conceal any longer, my time had come to say goodbye. I did not weep when I was forced to leave my home, nor when I said goodbye to my other ballerinas, nor when I stood on the stage of the opera house and realized I would never hear the raucous applause of the admiring rich any longer. I was empty of any thought, except of my child.

Once I became pregnant, and could not entertain them with my slim proportions, I was no longer useful to them. Disregarded like an outdated newspaper, a used broom, a cold cup of coffee—I went to Marie's flat.

Adette was born with white, wintery sunlight pouring through the one window of our tiny home, and her first cry pierced the early silence of a sweet Wednesday morning. She brought love with her, so much love that I cried upon seeing her—could not believe that I had ever considered a life without her in my arms, tried to imagine not feeling that heart-tearing love every day for the rest of my life, I was made complete by her presence.

Marie let us, my tiny little baby and me, have the bed for the first year of Adette's life. We sold some of my dresses to buy a worn out mattress that we shoved into a corner of the room, we cut some of my petticoats to clothe her for the first two years of her life, we sold my shoes so we could eat.

Eventually, I ran out of dresses to sell. During the night, when I was home cooing at Adette and watching her raven hair grow between moonlit dreams, Marie would work. She would pose on street corners, walk toward the nicer end of our side of town, and ask men if they would like to walk her home. Then she would go with them—wherever they wanted, do whatever they wanted, be whoever they wanted—for a while, and come back with less money than she should have made.

In the morning it was my turn. If it were warm, Marie would take Adette to the park with a blanket, she talked of gazing at the clouds and watching horses clop by, of napping together with the sunshine as their sheets. In the winter they went to cafes, huddled by the fireplace for warmth.

In the daytime, I went with men, brought them back to our flat, laid with them in the same spot my daughter was born, watched the lines in our ceiling move back and forth as they rocked against me. Thoughts of Monsieur Andre who had never asked me to call him names or call out a certain way. I wondered if a new ballerina was dabbing her neck with rose water, imagined Celeste wearing my silky robe and pulling her hair free of a rehearsal bun, as I had done so many times with few worries in my heart save for remembering if the third Rond de Jande in the allegro was en dedan or en dehors.

When Adette was fourteen—blue-eyed, with black hair that flowed in rivulets around her face like melted wax of a candle, too skinny and long-legged like her father, beautiful and kind like her mother—a man, Remy Quint, a frequent customer who was always friendly with me, offered me six times my usual asking price for the chance to have Adette's virginity.

"Let the girl decide for herself," Marie advised as she readied herself for work, drinking the last dregs of our weak tea as Adette snored on her aunt's bed. I sat at our scratched and battered roundtable, writing a letter before I would collapse onto my mattress on the floor and sleep until I had to wake up and do my day again.

"Out of the question," I told her before the door slammed shut behind her, my stomach growling, the bruises beneath my eyes darkening. Adette stirred but did not wake, and I continued to write.

Monsieur Andre answered my letter in person, a week after I had posted it. He looked out of place in the shadowy hall, clothes too fine and eyes too shifty in the cramped space. A younger man stood behind him.

"Madame Catherine Brisset." My name was a sigh as I opened the door to the flat. There were new wrinkles around his eyes, his once greying hair had been struck silver, the bags under his eyes were deeper and longer, and the sight of him made my palms sweat.

Beside him stood the man younger than Monsieur Andre but older than Adette, I supposed this made him close to my age—the age where women were forgotten, and men flourished.

Adette looked up from her place at the kitchen table, surprised by our guests. We didn't have many guests, and Adette had never seen a man in our home before.

"Please call me Catherine, Monsieur Andre Chaufourier." I greeted, sadness in my smile and understanding in Monsieur Andre's eyes as the men stepped into the flat.

"Then I must be Andre, in return."

When he swept down to kiss my cheeks, warm hands clutching my arms, he brought with him the aroma of tobacco and cognac mixed in the ocean of our memories.

He brought the Paris Opera Ballet into my little flat, squeezed the nerves of waiting in the wings, the discomfort of pointe shoes, my sore limbs soaking in the porcelain bath, the peaceful exhaustion that could come only from hours of dancing, his warm arms wrapped around me, the safety of our opulently decorated flat, into my new home.

I wondered how I seemed to him then, standing in stained clothing with dirty hair, surely fuller at the hips and thinner in the face than I had been when he had me.

"Catherine, allow me to introduce you to my colleague, Monsieur Henri Cabanel." Monsieur Andre's colleague was tall and blonde, with rosy lips and round cheeks topped with a pair of green eyes that curiously examined the room and my young daughter at the table.

"Madame Brisset."

"Monsieur Cabanel." He kissed my hand, and I was shocked to see the contrast in my tan skin against his pale hand. In all the years it had been since my ballet days, I thought I had managed to keep out of the sun, but it was obvious that I had failed.

"Gentlemen, allow me to introduce you to my daughter. Adette," She rose upon hearing her name, had been studiously watching our exchanges, smart enough to know when to appear shy and pretty to entrance men. She reminded me of me. "Adette, this is my old friend Monsieur Andre Chaufourier, he works at the Paris Opera Ballet. Andre, my daughter, Adette."

He bent, nearly in half, to kiss her hand. "A pleasure, Mademoiselle Brisset." I blanched to see her blush, watched as Andre's feathers were stroked before he turned to introduce his colleague, "This is Monsieur Henri Cabanel, he is in charge of directing our company in some of our productions this year. He has a place available for a ballerina."

"Would you have any interest in the Paris Opera, Mademoiselle Brisset?" Monsieur Cabanel asked, voice warm, eyes wandering over my daughter's figure.

"Oh yes, but I don't dance, monsieur." Adette was honest, enchantingly so. It would only help her in her new position, help her win friends, win assistance, win favor, win roles. She was beautiful. It pained me, it felt as if someone had skinned me raw, to know what she would do to win favor with men, it pained me that I would never see her dance on the stage, would never hear the boisterous applause of her admirers.

"A small hiccup in the grand scheme, Mademoiselle Brisset ... You strike me as a quick learner, do you mind me saying so?"

Adette had gasped and giggled, letting herself be led back to the kitchen table, a natural coquette with no training and no pretense. She would go far, I could see it in Monsieur Cabanel's appreciative gaze.

He handled her easily, a large hand resting on her shoulder, voice low and soft as he painted pictures of the opera house and the gorgeous crowds that gathered to see the shows there. The kind ballerinas she would dance with, and the extravagant costumes she would get to wear and the apartment he could get for her to stay in, all hers, with a private bath and all.

"Are you so sure about this?" Monsieur Andre asked me as we stood to the side, remaining by the door of the flat while Monsieur Cabanel wooed my daughter, seduced her out of my arms and into his own.

"No," I admitted, my eyes sliding up to meet his. There was pity there that I could not handle seeing, I had to look away, had to watch my daughter's cheeks fill with pleasure and heart flit away on dreams of praise and riches, "But I don't know a better way."

"Hmph." He smiled down at me, I could feel it and remember a hundred times before when he had done the same.

"Are congratulations in order?" I asked as Adette had slipped off her shoe and allowed her foot to fall into Cabanel's large hands so that he could show the proper way to turn out her leg, to point her toes, "Should I take Monsieur Cabanel's presence to mean that you have been promoted?"

"Ah yes, thank you. Henri is our newest director, he is very promising."

"Yes, I see."

Adette was laughing, taken with the enchanting, rich, polite gentleman who tickled the bottom of her foot and did not cringe at the dirt there. In a few months, she would look back, I was sure, and wonder what had made her so forward with a stranger, what would take hold of her to let her walk around in such filthiness. It would not be for years until she would forgive herself for her poverty, until she would be ashamed to meet me in public, until she would regret that I could not join her in polite society.

"It will be hard for you to say goodbye," Andre decided, his words finally allowing me to look away from my daughter making her agreement to become a woman.

"Yes, but it will be harder if she stays. It would be selfish of me to keep her here. There is nothing for her here, nothing that she can do but ..." *My work,* clear but unspoken, rested between us, wrapped around my lungs and brought embarrassment to my cheeks.

"Time is a curious thing. Your mother let you go, and yet you are back."

"I would not hope the same for Adette," I admitted.

"I doubt your mother wished this for you, either. Apologies, that was too forward—"

"No, no Andre, we are old friends. You know me well enough to know that what you say is true," I rested a comforting hand on his folded arms—still comforting him, accepting his apologies when I so badly needed the same. I squeezed there and remembered nights when those arms had clutched me to his body in our secret flat, safe away from the rest of the world, "It was the only thing my mother ever gave to me, but I was not brave enough to ... rid myself of circumstances that could have helped me escape ... I spit on my mother's gift."

Andre rested a hand over mine, and did not look away as he spoke sincerely, "You cherished mine."

Adette's laugh caught our attention, forced us to release our nostalgic hold on one another, we watched as Cabanel held out a pair of diamond earrings from his coat pocket. *My earrings.*

"Monsieur!" My darling little girl was delighted, she had never been so close to jewels before.

"Monsieur Andre found these not long ago, he says they used to belong to your mother."

"Is that true, maman?" Adette asked, hope winning over her confusion—*she had never seen me in my refinement, had never imagined her mother to have a life outside of the one that she knew me to have. How could I, a whore of the street who shared one room with both her sister and daughter, have ever worn diamonds?*

"It was a long time ago," I admitted, ever aware of my audience as I spoke, "before you were born. They will suit you better now, I think."

"Oh really, maman? Do you mean it?" She was sprinting toward me, leaving Cabanel staring after her, pulling me into a cheerful hug as I confirmed the gift. Giggling boisterously, she returned to Cabanel—only dismaying upon discovering that they were not earrings that she could clip on, her ears were unpierced. Andre watched me as she pouted, I could not return his stare.

"Well, we must have them pierced then!" Cabanel was quick to mollify her, not seeming aware of how easily Adette had beguiled him, of how quickly he had fallen for her. I wondered if he was married, I wondered if Adette would mind.

"Can I, maman?"

"You may do as Monsieur Cabanel advises, of course."

My daughter beamed, could not yet realize that I did not know if I was offering her up to the sheep or to the wolves. They returned to conversation, with Adette holding the diamonds carefully as she inspected them.

"You love her," Andre murmured.

"Yes, very much."

"She loves you." He assured me, and I nodded my agreement before he continued, "You are doing a very brave thing, you know this. You trust that I will look after her."

"Yes."

"I cannot keep Henri from having her," he warned, "it is just the way of things, always will be, I'm afraid."

"I hope you are wrong, but I understand. It is what is best," I watched as Cabanel held the diamond up to her ear, stroked dirty hair away from her lobe, "He's charming."

"More charming than I was."

"Yes, I think so."

"I wanted you so badly, I was brusque. It was unforgivable." I remembered his wandering hands well, the piercing of him on our first night together, the shame and confusion that had followed but had been bought away with a silver hairclip beaded with pearls, then the shame that followed that too.

"You took good care of me."

"Until I didn't."

"Yes. Yes, I suppose that is true." I was suddenly very tired, wanted little more than to turn back to a time when I could gather my toddler in my arms and cuddle her on our dingy mattress.

"So, we have an agreement then," Andre spoke to me after making short eye contact with Cabanel, "she will come with us, will train, will live as you once did. She'll be paid, but of course what she does with that money will be up to her."

The reality of his sentiments punched me in the gut, memories of a sweltering room and a young blonde woman pushing down on my bare belly sent shivers down my spine. I blinked, returning to the present where an older Andre stared at me, and my young daughter flirted with a man nearly double her age.

"When will you come back for her?" I whispered.

"Sunday."

"Three days?"

"I left with you the night of ... I thought I was being kind, I—"

"Yes, three days." I agreed, winning a grim nod of appreciation from the man who had once been my lover. Adette and I would go for a walk in the park, eat raspberries from the vendor that she found handsome, and talk about what to expect on her first night with Henri. I would do more for my daughter than my mother had done for me.

"Will you be okay?" Andre asked, "Is your sister around?"

"Yes, I will be fine."

"You're stronger than you think." He attempted a compliment but was rusty from all of our years of separation.

"Stronger than you know."

"Yes," We stopped watching Cabanel's fingers stroking our daughter's knee beneath the table, to smile at each other as my old beau agreed, "Yes, I dare say so."

The Allocated Bride

Dallas Alexander

If everything you've ever wanted comes to you, you take it, swish it around in your mouth, and spit it out. I never wanted for anything, for as long as I could remember. I grew up on the sunny side of the Barents Sea, Russia. My father owned more land than I could ever see in a lifetime and was a very famous sailor who turned his fortune by trading sea-faring for trades.

My life perhaps might have been perfect, if my mother would have survived giving birth to me and my father did not so often suffer from a disease that made his lungs weak. I was well accustomed to traveling with my father wherever his business ventures took him. I could sit and listen to him conduct entire business meetings, in multiple languages. I knew it was not my place to offer my opinions at the meetings, but sometimes he would ask me when the meetings were over, and even acted upon a suggestion or two on rare occasions.

When my father became quite ill that summer, we stayed in Florence while he was recovering. It was there that I met Pierre, a most handsome and spirited young man. He was altruistic, open-minded, and above all, he loved me. Countless nights we lay in a vineyard, suckling on grapes right from the vine and divining the stars.

It was our last night in Vienna that Pierre, and his elder brother Giuseppe, came to my father so that Pierre could ask for my hand in marriage.

"What say you, sir?" asked Pierre after he had made an affectionate and eloquent speech to my father about asking for my hand.

"No," said my father, without looking up from the map he was currently working on. My hand flew to my mouth in surprise.

"Father!" I pleaded, "Haven't you heard anything he's said?" I asked, grief-stricken. Pierre had more than gone over his affections, how he needed me more than the stars, how the earth itself would stand still before he let me go.

"Is that all?" asked my father to the brothers. Pierre looked pale, and I thought I might faint right there on the spot.

"Please, sir, is there anything I can do to persuade you?" asked Pierre meekly.

My father looked upset then. "As it stands, you have no money, no influence, and as the second sibling, no inheritance coming your way. Your brother, at least, I've heard about. He has wealth, a career ahead of him, and has made smart business investments. Perhaps if you learn from him for a few years, you may have a fool's chance ..." he said, and then was interrupted by a coughing fit which took him a moment to recover. Wiping his mouth with a handkerchief, he continued slower, "but as I said, as it stands now, the answer is no. I don't intend offense, but I would much rather see Valeria in the hands of your brother than in yours," he said crossly.

I sat down on a chair, scarcely believing what a turn of events this had come to. I had always believed that my father coveted my wishes and my love more than anything, and to see him so blatantly shove my deepest whims under the rug and into an eternity of darkness was too much. Nothing could be worse.

Giuseppe cleared his throat for a moment. He spoke softly, but with an air of authority.

"If that is your decision concerning my brother, sir, I would like to make a proposition of my own," I blinked slowly at him as if I might have heard him incorrectly.

My father sat back, looking intrigued.

"Valeria, please excuse us for a moment," said my father.

I blinked some more. Certainly, this wasn't my father. I was present for all of his business meetings, always! He looked pointedly at me, and I felt myself rising before my feet could begin to protest.

Pierre followed me out, sensing that this meeting was no longer inclusive of him either.

"What's happening?" I asked Pierre. I could feel my eyes pleading.

"Valeria, darling, please don't be upset. I asked my brother to do this, just in case your father refused me, so we could be together," he said, taking me into his arms.

"Asked him to do what?" I asked, in a horrified whisper.

"To marry you. Giuseppe approved, on agreed upon terms, of course," he said.

Agreed upon terms? What on earth is he playing at?

"I'm sorry my darling, that I couldn't speak to you about this sooner. I was terrified last night that your father would deny me and that I would have to watch you sail across the sea and never see you again. Now, today, I saw those fears realized, and I am so glad that I asked my brother for his help," he said and kissed my temple. "My dear, sweet Valeria."

I stood in complete shock for a moment longer before Giuseppe opened the door and looked at me. It was as if I was seeing him for the first time. I had seen him over the summertime, and again at picnics and lunches, we had been sailing together when Pierre wanted to take me to the island of Gorgona Scalo.

Where Pierre had short sandy sun-kissed hair, his brother had the opposite. Long, dark curls that he constantly had pulled back. Pierre had a long billowing white shirt and care-free brown trousers. Giuseppe always wore his business suit, with golden buttons and embroidered cuffs. He wore tight white uniformed pants and rather expensive looking boots. He was honestly the absolute opposite of Pierre, and I could hardly see where they were related, except their similar eyes, that reminded me of the white grapes we so often ate from each other's fingertips.

He tipped his hat to me and walked down the hallway. Pierre looked at his brother, who did not glance back toward us. He kissed me hastily and whispered, "tell me what your father says, my love. Either way, I'll meet you here tomorrow morning at first light. My light, my love," he said and kissed me again. Our fingers untangled as he called for his brother to wait up for him and I stood frozen in the hallway.

"Valeria," my father called softly. If I hadn't heard my own name my whole life, I might not have heard him at all. I felt like a sand flea, wanting desperately to dig myself into a little sandy hole after the waves have uncovered its hiding place. But I walked forward, like a ghost, and closed the door behind me. I couldn't bear to stand another step closer.

"Come here, cherry blossom," my father said, using my endearing nickname to goad me in like a small animal might be baited to the trap that snaps its neck.

"Father," I breathed, on the verge of tears. I didn't know what to say besides that, my thoughts too jumbled to coherently tell him what I was feeling. What was I feeling exactly? Not the hope I had in the beginning, or the despair after he had told Pierre no. This feeling was closer to fear, to anxiety, and ... heartache.

My father handed me his handkerchief. He had carried one for as long as I'd known him. It was embroidered along the edges with lavender; they were my mother's favorite flower. "Open it," he said softly, which wasn't what I was expecting.

When I did, I saw that there were specks, globules, smears of blood. I dropped it to the floor in shock, but I watched it flutter and land, still stained. I looked back at my father's face. That was the garment he had coughed into after telling Pierre he could not wed me.

"Father," I said again, feeling more like a child than ever, since I could not articulate what I wanted to tell him beyond that one word.

"I'm dying Valeria; I have been for a long time. I'm surprised I've been able to hold out as long as I have. I guess I have you to thank for that. Every day you grow more beautiful, the looking glass of your mother would not be able to tell the difference," he said. I trembled.

"And yet, the more you grow into her likeness, the more I miss her. I'll be glad to go, when it happens, if I have but a chance to see her again," he said.

I wanted to say something, but all I could come up with was, "Father ..." *He wants to abandon me, now of all times? Does he not think I miss my mother, the woman I didn't even have a chance to meet? Does he not believe that my love for Pierre is akin to what he felt for her?*

As if he could hear my thoughts he said, "I know that boy Pierre adores you darling, but he doesn't love you, as you might want to believe. And perhaps if he did, that might make all the difference," he said.

I wanted to tell him that Pierre did love me, but the words stuck in my mouth, because of what he had told me in the hallway. *Agreed upon terms.* I did not know what that meant. *Is Giuseppe to wed me and leave me here with Pierre? If that was his plan, it hardly seemed honorable. Did Pierre mean to share me with his brother?* I hoped to heavens that was not it. I refused in fact, to believe it. But I did not rise to his defense as I, just that morning, would have.

"Giuseppe has asked for your hand," he said, finally coming to his point, "and he has wealth, education, and property. He can take care of you far better than Pierre can. I have accepted his proposal, and your dowry will be arranged tomorrow before I sail back to Russia," he said.

He did not say 'we' would sail back. Tears, they were coming, and I tried to hold back the tide.

"And … if I say no?" I asked, knowing in my heart that it wasn't an option.

My father blanched at my words, knowing in turn that his response would be just as ghastly said aloud as it was in his own mind. Instead, he stayed silent, and we stared together at the candle that was slowly oozing wax upon his desk.

"Well, I've already packed," I said, my voice broke on the last word. My father stood up and embraced me while I sobbed into his arms.

—◈•◈—

I had dreamed of my wedding since I was a small child. There would be lanterns, dozens of people, lots of dancing and drinking, and no one would be frowning. Naturally, I'd have a dress that would be the envy of all others, and recently my dreams had Pierre and me in a vineyard.

The reality of my wedding was much different.

My father and Pierre were with me that morning as we entered a dress shop and purchased one that my father fancied. It did not suit me at all, it had too much lace, long sleeved, and had buttons up the front. At first, I thought it was strange that my father allowed Pierre to come. I had always thought that it was improper for the groom to see the bride in the dress, but then I remembered that Pierre was not going to be my groom, and the seamstress had the uncomfortable job of having to sew around my suffocating sobs.

That evening we climbed aboard my father's vessel, and it began to rain. The captain stood at the stern and Giuseppe looked at me through the veil as we stood hand in hand. Candles were held for us, shielded by others through the rain. Briefly, I looked over at Pierre, but he seemed to be happy, despite the circumstances, smiling brightly and encouragingly at me, which made me feel even more miserable.

The rings were blessed and placed upon our fingers, and we were given two crystal glasses to break. I smashed mine on the side of the deck with all of the energy I could muster. It broke into my hand, but I did not cry. I closed my hand around the wound.

The groom lifted my veil and placed a chaste kiss on my lips. I barely felt it. The entire procession clapped and cheered. I wanted nothing more than to run away crying.

My father came up to me then and placed an umbrella over me. He touched my chin, and I looked up at him.

"This was your mothers, it's yours now, my cherry blossom," he said, and placed a necklace of rubies in my uninjured hand. I looked at it in awe. "I love you," he said and kissed me on my cheek.

"I love you too, Papa," I said, and that was the last I saw of my father, as the procession was whisked away and swiped me from the deck.

Giuseppe, my husband, put his hand on the small of my back as he led me from the ship. Pierre was on our heels, as friends and family of theirs congratulated me. His mother and father took me in their arms and kissed both of my cheeks, promising to talk more at length when the weather wasn't trying to sweep us out to sea.

I smiled as best I could, which I know must have looked rather weak and strained.

I was nervous with every step away from the ship; I didn't even get to watch it sail away because we were running so swiftly from the rain. My dress was soaked, and it weighed heavily upon me, my heels were pressing themselves into the cobblestone and Giuseppe held tightly to me so whenever I slipped he could keep me upright.

Finally, we stopped, and I was out of breath, under the overhang of a very prestigious-looking hotel. It had an expansive lawn, fountains, and a rather impressive rose garden.

Pierre lived with his parents, and I didn't know where Giuseppe lived, but I didn't imagine it was in a hotel. I looked at him quizzically as we entered the lobby. He glanced down at me but didn't answer the question I knew he saw in my eyes. Instead, we reached the receptionist, who was smoking and looking over a magazine. When she looked up over her half-moon spectacles, she smiled appreciatively. I frowned at her, but she didn't seem to notice.

"Mr. Valspar, always a pleasure, would you like your regular room?" she asked, and then as if seeing us for the first time, glanced over at us appreciatively as well.

Whatever is this about?

"No thank you, Liza, a two-bedroom will due for the night," he said. For a minute, I thought he meant one for Pierre and me, and another for him, or maybe the brothers in one room and I would be in another? He looked at me, and his gaze was heated. I then suspected neither of those scenarios was the case.

We had to walk up a flight of stairs, which only exhausted me further. I had to stop halfway, and they waited for me patiently on the landing while I mustered the strength, physically and mentally, to make it.

When Giuseppe opened the door, I wanted to find the nearest bed and fall into it, but I had better manners and held myself in check. I was living the fine line between being scared for my life and ready to sink like a stone. I stared at the wooden floor, where my dress was dripping steadily and making a puddle.

Without asking, Giuseppe started to untie the corset from behind me. I stilled, like an animal caught in the teeth of its prey. I felt like a canary, my heart pattering behind the cage that was my ribs. The soaked corset fell down to the floor, and I took a deep breath. I was shivering.

"Did you pack extra clothes?" asked Giuseppe.

I nodded silently and looked in the corner where Pierre had deposited my suitcase. It too was developing its own puddle.

Giuseppe looked crossly at Pierre who shrugged. "Can you manage to undress, grab a blanket and let us know when you're ready? Then we'll return to discuss our arrangement," said Giuseppe. He looked at Pierre, who looked at me rather hopefully, before following his brother into the next room.

I felt like I was not myself as I unbuttoned the rest of my dress, removed my garters, hose, and panties, unlaced my boots, and peeled off my socks, all of them sodden with water.

I stopped when I wrapped a thin blanket from the mattress around me and sat, feeling very vulnerable.

"I'm ready," I whispered, almost a clear indication that I was anything but, yet they must have had their ears pressed to the door because they somehow heard me and were both standing there staring at me.

"First," Giuseppe said, "I want you to know that we are now legally married Valeria. I am under no obligation to enter into an agreement other than the one we both swore an oath to this evening, to each other," he added for emphasis. "But," he continued, "I also made certain promises to my brother, and I take my word very seriously. I'll ask you to hear what he has to say," he said.

Pierre scowled at his brother briefly, and began, "Valeria, my light, this was the only way, as I told you before. We can be together now. Your father is gone; he's in no position to halt our love. My brother has agreed that we may be together for the weekdays, and you'll be his on the weekends. Also, that his wedding night would be sacred, which I agreed to," he said.

Agreed upon terms. I had hoped, when he had talked about terms, that he meant that his brother would sail away, or get a divorce, something clever that would have us living the rest of our lives alone together. *But this?*

I didn't think I had ever felt this before, not in my whole seventeen years, had I felt ... hatred. Hot, white, solid, heavy, boiling, hatred. *He is planning on sharing me with his brother. What does he think our love is?*

I looked at Pierre, as if for the first time. His skin was kissed by the sun, his clothes loose-fitting and although wet, comfortable and soft. *Soft, that is what he is, his fingers when he tucked my hair, his lips when he kissed me in the vineyard, his mind when he thought I would ever, ever stand for such a ludicrous idea.*

The only hope I had left, ironically, stood in a soaked suit. He had asked that I listen, not that I had to accept the terms.

"And, if I say no?" I asked. This time, I would not stand meekly by as I had when I asked my father. I demanded to know what would happen. I had to hear it out loud.

Pierre looked shocked, as if in his innocent, idealistic world, such an outcome would never happen. Just as he didn't think that my father would refuse him.

"Then Pierre will be escorted back to my parent's villa. I have the staff ready, whatever you decide," he said.

My shoulders relaxed at that. Now I had to hear aloud, what Giuseppe thought, though I supposed I already knew. "And, if it were up to you?" I asked Giuseppe, looking him in the eyes so he could not mistake who my question was directed to. It was the first time that I saw the hint of a smile on him, so bright and fleeting, it made my heart flutter again, in a completely different way.

"If it were up to me, Pierre would've waved goodbye from the rearview of my parent's stagecoach," he said. Pierre looked at his brother incredulously.

"I think ... Pierre, you should go home," I said, both terrified and sound at the same time. Giuseppe looked at his brother and Pierre couldn't stop looking at me.

"Valeria, my light," he said.

"No," I said, and I couldn't even gaze upon him.

"Look at me," he pleaded.

"Brother," said Giuseppe, "I think my wife has asked you to leave," he said.

I could almost feel Pierre bristle.

"You planned this, didn't you? You *bastardo*, this isn't the end, Valeria is just confused, in shock," he said.

"Even still," said Giuseppe.

Pierre stepped forward, I saw his shoes move, and I turned my whole body away from him.

"I'll be back tomorrow, love, first light okay?" he said sweetly. I nodded, just to register I'd heard him. He took his time, moving slowly, and when the door closed behind him, Giuseppe secured it.

I waited, a little terrified for a while, as the silence dragged on.

"Valeria," said Giuseppe.

I looked up at him through my lashes.

He paused. Perhaps now that we were finally alone together, he was having second thoughts.

I was a royal wreck. I shivered under the covers, awaiting his decision.

"Are you cold?" he asked me.

I nodded.

"I'll run you a bath," he said quietly, but it was full of masculinity. I watched him walk to the bathroom and heard the faucet. He appeared a few moments later at the doorway. "It's ready," he said.

I stood up, the blankets still draped around me, and I walked to the bathroom.

Once inside I turned around, waiting for him to leave and close the door behind him, but he stayed just as he was. I let the blankets drop and stepped into the tub. I couldn't help the sound of pure bliss that escaped my lips as the water warmed my flesh. I sunk deep into the tub and looked at him as he closed the door and sat on the commode.

I felt very self-conscious of him staring at me and my cheeks heated under his stare.

"Please, pretend I'm not here. I just want to watch you," he said. I took the soap on the loofah and proceeded to scrub my arms, my belly, my breasts, and legs. After a while, I was less conscious of his gaze and more concerned with my bath.

Without looking at Giuseppe, I asked, "What is going to happen later?" he put a hand under his chin, as if in deep thought.

"I think, we'll talk a little, I'll order room service, and at some point, we'll consecrate our marriage," he said.

I blushed harder, thinking about it. In my culture, women didn't lie with a man until they were married. I always thought that man would be Pierre, but I found out today that would not be the case. The sting of that information was still quite a sore subject.

"And then tomorrow?" I asked, still not quite able to muster the strength to look at him. Pierre said he would be coming at first light, and I very much dreaded seeing him.

"I'll be taking you to my ship before dawn, and we'll set sail along the coast, I have some business to attend to, but if you'd like we could stop at beach for a day or two," he said.

"Before first light?" I asked and looked up at him.

"Yes."

"What about Pierre?"

"What about him?" he replied. I giggled in the bath, imagining his face tomorrow when he found out we had departed and not waited to say goodbye.

Giuseppe stood up and removed his clothes. I stared at his naked form in awe for a moment, he had hair, thick curls of it, on his chest, legs, and pubic area.

"Scoot over," he whispered. I made room for him to sit behind me and he pulled me up onto his chest, the water sloshing over the sides of the tub. I was quite frozen in his grasp as he slowly played with strands of my hair.

"I want to wash this," he asked, pulling lightly.

"What if I say no?" I said, breathlessly. He poured a cup-full of water over my head, and I gasped and laughed.

"Life is meant to be enjoyed Valeria, and you've already learned that I don't take no for an answer," he said lightly.

I smiled to myself as he dribbled soap into his fingers and began to massage my scalp.

The Prince of The Forest

Leslie D. Soule

Prince Roderick ran a trembling hand through his thick black hair as he awaited his mother's return. He did not want to go into the Old Forest, long-believed to be haunted and enchanted. *What if I just say no?* He pondered the thought. *Surely, she'll not force me to go. After all, it's the 16th century, and times have changed ... a Prince had more freedom these days than in centuries past.*

He paced across the room and took a seat in a simple wooden chair by the window. The rain drizzled down the glass and the Prince sighed. *Father is punishing me for not finding a suitable wife to produce heirs.* Revolutions threatened to collapse the royal House of Habsburg as the people of Hungary grew steadily dissatisfied with their government. Roderick propped his elbows onto his knees and settled his head into his hands. The King had given him an errand.

"Why should I have to be the one to speak with commoners? Is our Kingdom so poor that we cannot hire tax collectors? I have better things to do."

A mighty crack of thunder shook the sky, and the rain fell steadily harder. The door creaked open on rusty hinges, leaving Queen Emese standing in its frame.

"Roderick, my son, you look so crestfallen. I know it's raining, but if you take your cloak, you should manage to stay fairly dry."

Roderick stood up. "Mother, why have I been given this task?"

"Pardon?" She crossed the room and removed her bonnet, allowing rich brown curls to cascade down her shoulders.

"Father has sent me on a useless errand to go and meet up with that crazy, one-eyed old witch who lives in the forest and to collect taxes from her. Why must I go? Do we not have tax collectors?"

The Queen simply shrugged and said, "Perhaps he is testing you."

Roderick found himself momentarily taken aback by this strange thought. "Testing me? Whatever do you suppose he'd be testing me for?"

"I don't know, darling," the Queen replied. She took a cloth napkin from the table and unfolded it. Then she covered the wicker bread basket that sat nearby. She crossed the room and stood before Roderick, holding the basket out in front of her. "Do be a dear and deliver these to Borbala when you go."

Roderick accepted the basket, pinching the cloth between two fingers and gently lifting it to spy on the basket's contents.

Within, two small loaves of bread sat nestled next to one another.

So now I am to be a courier as well as a tax collector.

"I will, mother," he obediently replied as her emerald eyes bored into his.

"Do not be too harsh," she advised. "Life has been difficult for Borbala. She lost her husband in that accident so many years ago, after all."

The Prince fumed. "That does not exempt her from the King's law." *The common folk will not behave so defiantly when I am King.* He'd already started forming plans for crushing the peasant uprisings.

An attendant knocked on the door.

"You may enter," said Roderick.

A young man with a head of tight black curls and beady mouse eyes entered, his gaze full of intensity as it darted around the room. "My liege, your horse is ready,"

"Thank you, Mathias. I will be right out."

Mathias led Roderick's horse from the stables. The heavy hooves of Stormchaser clapped the ground like thunder strikes. Roderick climbed into the saddle and then adjusted his heavy black cloak. Stormchaser whinnied. Unlike his name, he did not seem to like the rain that now poured down in a relentless torrent.

"It's alright, ol' boy," said Roderick reassuringly. "I don't like it either. The sooner we meet up with that old crone, the sooner we can get you back in the stables." *And the sooner I can settle in by a nice hot fire.*

Roderick and Stormchaser followed the lesser road leading away from Castle Habsburg and away from the direction of the city. Their destination was a part of the forested area between the Volga River and the Ural Mountains. This morning, the rain carried with it the heady scent of smoke.

The clouds began to grow slightly lighter in hue as they unburdened themselves of rain. Roderick liked to believe that it was because he rode Stormchaser—that the horse's might had intimidated the very storm clouds from the sky, intimidating them into non-existence, in keeping with his name.

They turned off onto a gravel pathway and continued on. Oaks grew more numerous as they headed into the forest.

A wolf's howl echoed through the woods. Rain dripped from the dark canopy as Roderick's steed trotted down the gravel-lined pathway leading further in. Roderick had never traveled to this part of the forest before.

At last, he spotted a small thatched house, tucked away amongst the oaks. His breath caught in his throat as he spied the gleaming white skull of a fox, secured above the door. The Prince rode closer and then dismounted. Once he tied his horse's reins to an oak, he approached the hut. His boots crunched leaves and twigs with every step. *They break beneath my feet, just as this silly peasant uprising will when I become King and seize control of Castle Habsburg. The treasury of Hawk's Castle will simply sing with taxed gold.*

He rapped sharply on the shoddy wooden door. "Open this door at once, Cili Borbala, in the name of the Prince." The door swung open, revealing an elderly one-eyed woman with an eye patch.

"Ah, Prince Roderick. Come, sit." She gestured for the Prince to come inside.

Within, a crackling fire burned with a cooking pot suspended above it. The Prince caught the aroma of stew, and it made his mouth water. *But I've come on business,* he reminded himself.

"I cannot," he replied. He handed her the basket laden with bread. "However, my mother, Queen Enese, wishes you to have these loaves of bread."

Borbala accepted the basket. "Your mother is a kind woman."

Roderick was the sort of person who didn't take compliments well, whether they were directed at himself or a member of the royal family. So he now chose to dodge that particular compliment and delve into the heart of the matter at hand."

"She is, and her kindness has been ill-reciprocated by your refusal to obey the laws of taxation. As you know, our Kingdom is attempting to deal with the uprisings that have spread like wildfire throughout all of Europe. We lack the funding to continue for long, and thus the taxation laws must be obeyed." He paused and then produced a scroll from his leather satchel. "According to our records, you have not paid taxes in over ten years. It is this sort of behavior that threatens the Kingdom's viability."

Borbala shook her head. She gestured toward a sprig of lavender that hung above the door. "I provide herbs to the people and heal the sick. You want that I should pay you to provide these services to the people?" She laughed. "What kind of sense does that make?"

Prince Roderick felt his cheeks flush with heat. He had never dealt with such a brazen display of insolence. He raised his voice and practically shouted, "You have been warned. You have until the week is out to pay back the total of your due, or armed soldiers will be sent here to force you out of the Kingdom!"

Borbala simply laughed. "You act like you are King. But ... you will not be King. You lack compassion."

"You do not need compassion in order to rule. All you need is strength."

"Then that is all you shall have. You think it is so easy to just pack up and leave. I will root you to the ground. But your mother's kindness has not gone unnoticed. For this, I grant her son a boon of mercy, that he shall, for two hours a day, one for each loaf of bread, have the freedom and beauty of a dove."

"Crazy old witch," Roderick muttered, taking off his leather gloves. *You're lucky the law forbids me from strangling old witches and leaving them to die in the forest.*

Then she began chanting in words that the Prince could not understand. Though he wanted to turn and leave, he found that he could not. Prince Roderick stood transfixed by Borbala's single violet eye. He clutched his chest, feeling a strange, sudden burning there.

His hands shook and the skin of his arms visibly darkened. His feet felt heavy, like leaden weights. With great difficulty, he took a step, his foot sinking into the dirt. Tears welled up in his eyes, and his throat became parched. His skin wrinkled up like an old man's, as though the moisture had been instantly taken from it.

"What is happening to me?" he asked aloud. His horse became spooked and fought against the reins that held it tied to a tree. He felt taller. A creaking sound issued from his bones as his legs and arms elongated. He screamed as the transformation took effect, and the solitary scream became the whistling of wind through the leaves. Old Crazy-Eye Borbala had transformed Prince Roderick into just another tree of the forest.

Because of his mother's kindness, Borbala's spell allotted the Prince two hours a day in which he lived the life of a snowy white dove. Though he'd heard rumors about Borbala and her witchcraft, he hadn't seen proof until now. Now, the evidence was beyond dispute. The first few days of his new existence, he spent his two dove hours in lamentation.

He flew toward the direction he'd come from. Unaccustomed to flight, he found it to be both awkward and exhilarating. He also felt exposed in a new sort of way. Being a Prince meant that his life became a spectacle for public display, every aspect observed and scrutinized. Yet he'd never felt this particular manifestation of vulnerability. *Where did my clothes go?* He supposed that they must have transformed along with his body.

A hawk glared at him as it sat perched on the branch of an oak. The Prince glared back, forgetting his size. Then he flew as fast as his little wings would allow. The hawk began its pursuit, issuing a sharp battle cry as it rode the air currents.

Fear consumed Roderick. He did not know what type of bird he had been turned into, but guessed it to be a dove. He'd been transformed into something small and white. His heart beat quick as a horse's hooves in a race. *Sir Thomas's rookery!* Rooks hated hawks. He'd seen them gang up on a lone hawk on many a hunt. Sir Thomas raised large, aggressive rooks. *If I can only make it to the rookery, I may yet be saved.*

Roderick spotted a dark spot in the sky and knew that he'd be saved. The sky became sprinkled with pepper as crows left the rookery and went on the warpath. *Onward! Onward!* He urged his little wings to carry him further toward safety, toward the rookery.

He dared not look behind him, though his heart experienced torrents of joy each time one of Sir Thomas's menacing crows jolted past.

A crowd had gathered in the town square. The church bells thundered as Prince Roderick shot through the sky, desperately seeking the protection of crows.

He landed on the signpost of the town's haberdashery. Though he never shopped there himself, he'd heard of the shopkeeper's nearly encyclopedic knowledge of all things fashion. In the store window, a display of brightly colored silk handkerchiefs invited the gazes of onlookers.

Roderick perched close enough that he could hear the old shopkeeper converse with one of his patrons.

"The royal family's been killed, King, Queen, even Prince Roderick, all dead."

The Prince could not believe what he heard. He'd lost both his father and mother at once! No one knew where he was, and so they supposed him to be dead, too. The thought of it all was too much to bear. His mind reeled with the implications.

He didn't know whether he ought to fly to Castle Habsburg and seek out proof, or to risk flying back into the woods, or whether he'd rather just sacrifice himself to the hungry hawk that had pursued him thus far. He searched the pit of his soul and what he found there surprised him. In his princely days, he'd been involved in duels with sharpened rapiers, he'd hunted wild boars armed with only a dagger and a bit of luck, he'd talked back to his mother, bold as ever. Yet somewhere deep down, he feared death in all its terrifying power.

Thus, he could not sacrifice himself to the hawk. He would not fly quietly and complacently into the beak of death. *No*, he decided. *I will find that witch, Borbala, and spy on her with the time I have while I'm a dove.*

He looked over at the clock tower, unsure how much time had passed. He wondered if he would change into a tree where he stood and determined that landing on the ground and waiting would probably be wise. So, he flew to a deserted spot behind a building and landed on the ground. A breeze blew and brought with it the faint salty scent of a distant ocean shore. It made his heart grow heavy with the realization that he'd lost so much freedom due to his enchantment.

A warm tingling sensation began to form. It started under his wings and then covered them entirely, spreading over the dove's body like a hot aura. Prince Roderick closed his eyes, for he felt that he could keep them open no longer. The aura spread to his insides, as though a fire had formed there, pulsing out and then back in.

When he opened his eyes, he saw that he'd been transported back to the woods and transformed into a tree once more.

So, the next day, Roderick eagerly awaited the coming of sunrise. As soon as the rays of the morning sun fell onto his bark, it filled him with a sense of hope and purpose. He closed his eyes, and the hot sensation enveloped him. When he opened them, he stood perched on a branch. Then he darted off into the air, not wanting to waste a moment of his precious freedom.

He scoured the forest for an hour and found nothing. He wondered if the old witch had simply packed up and left, taking with her the secrets of her magic. If this were the case, he knew he'd be doomed to the unnatural sort of life he'd inadvertently signed up for. *I must map out the forest somehow ... find a way to mark the areas I've already searched. There must be a way, and yet, ideas now forsake me.*

Johanna held fast to the handle of the carriage door as she stood outside of it, on the leather-covered boot step reserved for servants. Her knuckles were white, and every bump in the road sent a fresh jolt of terror down her spine. She knew nothing of politics and would certainly not be invited into the royal household. She rode along at the request of Lady Kamala, who wished to purchase dresses for her daughter Bernadette on the return trip. Johanna would help the Lady Kamala to choose amongst the various fabrics and designs.

The lantern shined onto a great pit in the middle of the dirt road. The carriage shuttled along too fast to avoid it. The horse whinnied and crashed along with the carriage.

She saw the carriage begin to tumble over and leapt backward, out of harm's way, landing on a soft cushion of leaves by the side of the road. Fear led her to quickly pick herself off the ground and run to hide behind the nearest tree. From there, she watched in horror as the lantern slipped from its spot beside the driver and crashed to the ground, simultaneously setting its spilled oil ablaze and lighting up the dark figures of a duo of bandits.

As she peered out from behind the tree, she saw the forms of two riders dressed all in dark clothing. Johanna tucked herself further behind the tree. Bandits! She'd heard of such people but never encountered them before. She wanted to scream, but terror stopped her voice, and she silently prayed for her life. A shot rang out into the night and Johanna inadvertently jumped.

One of the bandits paused. "Did you hear something?"

Johanna stood as still as a statue. She dared not even breathe.

"Naw," said one of the bandits. "We're just hearin' things."

She heard Lady Kamala scream and then heard the driver, old Mr. Carrington, plead for mercy. Johanna desperately wished that she could help them, but she feared death at the hands of the bandits. She sat stock still, cloaked in the darkness of the night and concealed by the oak.

"Heh, here's a pretty hat," said one of the men. Johanna could not believe the inhumanity of what she was hearing. Tears streamed down both cheeks as she suppressed the burning desire to scream out.

Then she listened in horror as the two men unloaded the chambers of their revolvers.

Murder! The blood instantly chilled in her veins. She knew she must tell someone, alert the authorities, but she was miles and miles from the nearest town. She dared not travel the roads all alone at night, especially by foot. Innumerable dangers lurked there, waiting for young women like Johanna, who had no source of protection. She would have to stay where she was and spend a night all alone in the dark woods.

She waited for many hours before she dared to move or speak, not knowing how long the murderers might linger before moving on. She could not bring herself to look toward the road or to think about examining the horrible spectacle that would await her there. She looked up into the sky and saw the moon glowing, imagined it being a protective celestial force, a beacon of light in the cold, dark forest.

A fresh wave of grief washed over her as she considered the dread fate that would surely come. "What can a poor girl like me do now? I do not know how to survive in the forest. No human being, who could help me find food, lives in it, so I must certainly starve."

"My dear, do not cry. All is not yet lost."

Upon hearing the sound of a human voice, Johanna looked up into the branches of a tree. She saw no one. Only a dove sat perched upon a branch above her.

She had never known birds to speak in the voices of human beings. Now that she heard it, she wondered if she were only dreaming. Perhaps this had all been nothing more than a horrible nightmare.

She was overjoyed at the possibility that none of this was real. She'd wake up in her familiar old cot, and Lady Kamala and Mr. Carrington and the horse would all be alive.

She closed her eyes and leaned back against a tree, trying to fall asleep. Then she waited. A cold breeze hit her cheek, distracting her from the important task at hand. Sleep would not come.

The moonlight glinted at the bird's breast, and the creature quit its perch to fly onto her shoulder. She looked over and saw that a tiny key hung on a golden cord around the dove's neck.

"Take this key from me. Then find a tree, any tree will do, even this one. Knock three times and the tree spirit will awaken to protect you from the misfortune that has befallen you."

Gingerly, she slipped the cord from the bird's neck. The key felt heavy in her palm, much heavier than it looked. She wanted to believe that benevolent forest spirits might protect her. The thought of spending a night all alone in the woods made her blood run cold. So, she knocked on the oak three times, and on the third, she gasped. A golden metal lock materialized, and the wood cracked, forming the semblance of a door.

"The tree spirit has heard you," said the dove. "Go on, try the key in that little lock."

Though she did not know how such miraculous things could be real, Johanna could not deny what she saw. With a trembling hand, she inserted the tiny golden key into the lock and turned. A click resounded through the woods, and as she pulled upon the key, the tree's door opened outward on its hinges. A ray of silvery moonlight illuminated the silhouette of a bed within, and Johanna's tears began anew.

"How can I ever repay you?" she asked. The dove said nothing. It only cooed and flew away into the night.

After a full night's rest, Johanna opened her eyes. From inside, the oak tree seemed so much larger than it looked on the outside. Her stomach grumbled, and she glanced around her room. To her left stood a wooden dresser with a painting sitting on top, propped against the wall. The image appeared to be a young woman who looked very much like herself but in fancy clothes. Behind her stood a tree, in the process of metamorphosizing into a man. The man held the woman's gaze and with his hands, gently grasped her arms.

Johanna wondered what the curious image meant. She pulled out all four drawers of the dresser but found them to be completely empty. Her stomach again rumbled, this time more fiercely. "I must find food soon," she mumbled.

As she exited the tree room, she looked up into the canopy. On a low branch, she spotted a white dove. "Could it be the same one from before?" she asked the forest.

"My dove," said Johanna, "are you my dove?"

After a moment's silence, the dove spoke. "Did you sleep well, my dear? Is there anything further that you require?"

"Yes," Johanna replied. "I slept better last night than I have in years. And I'm doing well, it's just ... I'm a bit hungry. Do you know where I can find some food?"

"Yes. You must take that same key and go to a different tree than the last. This time, knock twice and then enter."

"Oh, thank you, my dove," Johanna replied. The dove had once again found a way to protect her. Again, she asked, "How can I ever repay your kindness? Alas, I am a poor servant girl and cannot buy you anything in return."

"My dear," cooed the dove, "Money does not buy you anything when you are in the woods."

"And that we are," replied Johanna.

"Along with all of mankind, my dear." With that, the dove flew off, leaving Johanna alone once more with the little golden key.

"I wish I were a dove," she said. "Then I could escape this wretched fate. How long can I possibly hope to live in this forest?"

She found another oak. This one looked nearly as slender as the old broom she used in her servant duties. "There is no way that a room will open up inside. The tree is much too thin for that," she said.

She knocked twice, and this time, a silver lock appeared. She inserted the key and turned until she heard it click. A crack appeared in the tree and extended beyond it, into the ether. The form of the door took up both tree and ether, as though reality had become the illusion of this strange forest. She pulled upon the key, and the door opened to reveal a massive inner chamber with a table large and grand enough for a King and all his servants. Bowls of ripe red apples tempted Johanna, and her nose became bombarded with delicious scents. A glazed, honeyed ham sent waves of heat into the air. Her mouth began to water.

When Johanna had eaten her fill, she left the tree and searched the forest for the one that held her room, but to no avail. She did not remember which tree she'd first found.

"Oh, why didn't I leave some sort of mark?"

Just then, a strange thought occurred to her. "Perhaps, well perhaps it doesn't have to be a certain, specific tree." She spied a white birch tree and knocked upon it three times. A sense of relief washed over her as the golden lock appeared. As soon as she entered, she collapsed onto the bed and fell into a deep slumber.

Johanna lived like this for some time, traveling between her bedroom and the banquet hall. Every morning, the dove would perch on her shoulder and sing her a song. Then it would leave, and Johanna did not know where it went or why it could not stay.

Johanna sat down on a stump as she tried to recall memories from before she came into Lady Kamala's household. If she really tried, she could picture her mother's bright blue eyes and remember her mother brushing through her long flaxen hair. She never knew her father. Her mother died of a rare medical condition, leaving Johanna utterly alone and orphaned. At the age of six, Johanna found herself bereft of hope and future. Though she lived in Lady Kamala's household, Johanna had the sort of love apportioned to hired help and not that afforded to daughters.

For much of her life, she'd felt rather alone. So being in the woods by herself, with no one for comfort while her dove was away, was like a return to normalcy.

She had heard the tunes of other birds, and though she wanted to believe that perhaps some of them had been granted the gift of speech, she'd found none with that gift besides her dove. So she sang songs that she remembered and took long strolls through the woods. She could barely fathom the idea of leading such a carefree life that she'd be free from servant duties and toil for the rest of her days.

The light filtered down through the forest canopy and rays of golden sunshine alighted on mossy trunks, on ferns and grasses, on stones and reeds. She sang a graceful, lilting tune and watched a bright red dragonfly flutter past. Without any watches or clocks, she had no way of knowing the time of day, not that it mattered. Life in the woods meant that the minutes and hours and days all melded into one another to form the raw material of a carefree existence.

As she realized that her needs were being provided for, a sense of comfort began to work its way over Johanna and to lessen the damage of the things that had been done. The only thing she wished for was a companion to share her days with. But the only men she'd encountered had been visitors to the household. She knew men to be brutish creatures ruled by their appetites. But she dreamed of a man who held compassion in the depths of his heart.

Maybe he'd find her, and she could conceal her past life as a member of the peasantry. Her fine new clothes would certainly disguise her well enough and allow her to look the part of a higher social class. She sighed.

One day, she happened upon a young fox cub by the side of the road. Its mother had been hit by a carriage in the middle of the night. So, she swaddled the little creature in the folds of her dress and took it with her into the woods. She looked around cautiously, fearing she might run into the carriage robbers again, but she saw no one. As she turned to walk back into the woods, she saw the symbol of a key, burned into the bark of an oak tree. The symbol was oddly comforting, as it reminded her of the little golden key that her dove had given her. This key had kept her safe and secure in the otherwise frightening and intimidating forest.

Yet her clothes grew steadily more ragged as the days wore on. So, she asked the little dove, "Do you know where I may find some clothes? My own have grown so worn."

So, the dove instructed her, "You must take that same key. Go to a tree and knock once this time. Therein, you shall find clothing."

Johanna found a suitable tree and this time, knocked only once. This time, a bronze lock appeared. When she used the key and entered, a stunning sight revealed itself. Within, racks of clothing stretched the length of a dining hall. She found dresses of silk and satin, ball gown with delicate embroidery and garments adorned with jewels. These clothes seemed far more splendid than those of any King's daughter. Johanna had never worn such finery.

One morning, the dove said to Johanna, "Will you do something for me?"

"With all my heart," Johanna replied.

"What I ask you to do is dangerous. Deep in these woods, there is a small house where a witch lives. I ask you to enter, but you must not speak to her if she is inside. One word from you will give her power over you, for she steals the very stuff of voices. I will lead you to her house, and there instruct you further, if you will still go."

"I owe you my life, my dove," she replied. "I will go."

The dove flew ahead of her and led her through the rush of trees. Johanna jogged at a brisk pace as she dodged trees and boulders. She traveled a trackless path, on and on until she felt the burn of exertion stinging in both legs. Finally, she spotted a house and slowed to a steady walk. The dove flew down and landed on her shoulder.

"Now, my dear one, when you enter the house, remember not to say a word. This is very important. Whatever the woman says to you, you must not reply. Once you are inside, you should see a door leading to a back room. Open this door and enter. Somewhere within will be a quantity of rings of various size and expense. Some of them will be magnificent rings with shining stones, rings worth more than all the Kingdom, yet you must leave them be. Somewhere, there is a plain copper ring, and it is this one which you must seek. Once you have it, bring it to me as quickly as you can."

"I will do this for you, my dove," said Johanna.

"Thank you," replied the dove. "Good luck, my dear one." The dove flew over to a nearby tree and hid his head beneath his wing. Johanna saw a single, crystal-clear tear fall and splash upon the branch.

Johanna gripped the little golden key in her hand as she approached the door of the house. A candle flickered in the window, and so Johanna supposed that the old woman must be home. She took a deep breath as she ascended the porch stairs. Crossing the porch, she gripped the cold doorknob and twisted. She opened the door and spotted the old woman sitting in a rocking chair in front of a crackling fire. The old woman wore an eye patch. She turned to look at Johanna, who refused to meet her gaze, meekly staring at the floorboards instead as she entered.

"Good day, my child," said the old woman.

Say nothing, Johanna reminded herself. *Oh, but it seems so rude. Yet I must obey my dove, after all he has done for me.*

"Indeed?" said the old woman. "You enter my house and then have nothing to say?"

Johanna nodded and kept walking, tightly clutching the golden key. She reached the door in the back and gripped its knob, glancing behind her. The old woman merely sat, staring into the flames.

Within, Johanna found the room to be empty except for a round wooden table with a red velvet tablecloth. Its surface lay covered in rings that glittered and gleamed. She had never seen such wealth in all her life, not even in Lady Kamala's grand estate. The sight enticed her. *If I take one of these rings and sell it, I could live like a noblewoman for the rest of my days.*

She picked up one of the rings and examined it. In its center sat a ruby the color of blood, large as a marble. She lifted the ring up to the light and turned it, examining the way the rays reflected off its surface. *I could easily slip away with a few. That woman surely won't notice. I could live in comfort for the rest of my days.* Then she tried it on and held up her hand, admiring the way it looked there. She glanced behind her at the window. Sitting there on the sill beyond it, her dove cried another crystal tear. Its words echoed in her memory, "You must leave them be."

"Oh, I am coming," said Johanna. "What a fool I've been! I don't know why a dove would ever want a ring, what a silly thing, but I will get it for him."

She pushed all of the rings into a massive pile in the center of the table. Then she sighed, realizing how long the task of sorting would take. *Yet if I never start, I'll never finish.*

She picked up a golden ring with three round diamonds and set it to the side. Then, she plucked an emerald ring and set it aside as well. As she continued, a curious thing happened. The wealth of the rings began to lose its hold on her. She started to realize that she'd been under the old witch's spell for so long, the fetishism of wealth. This task proved it. She became mentally disgusted with herself and this sense of distaste radiated into her hands. She worked faster and faster, no longer setting the fancy rings into neat little piles. Now she tossed them about haphazardly.

When she encountered one, she treated it with the mercy given to a parasite. The floor became littered with priceless rings as Johanna sought out the plain one among them. She would not fail her dove.

Eventually, she found the copper ring and slipped it onto her finger so she wouldn't lose it, for she felt that her task would not be fully completed until she'd thrown every single expensive ring to the floor.

This task finished, she returned to the main room. Smiling, she looked at the old woman, who hissed and shrieked but could do no more. Johanna silently exited. Once outside, she searched frantically for her dove, scanning the canopy and peering up into the empty branches of innumerable trees. She ran to the back of the house but found the windowsill empty. She ran through the woods, scanning the treetops. Finally, weary with exhaustion, she leaned against the trunk of an oak.

She felt a warmth emanate from the tree and its branches seem to sink and become pliant. Then the branches twined around her. She saw them change into two arms. Whirling around, she saw that the tree had become a handsome man. The man scooped Johanna into his arms.

"My dear one," he said, "I am thy dove."

"Oh, my dove, I love you," she replied and then kissed him ardently, for she didn't know how long this strange magic might last.

"Did you notice the locks?" he asked her. "They appear that way for a reason, you know. The metals represent the value of that which is contained therein. These beautiful clothes ... they are nothing without an equally beautiful soul to wear them. Food is of no use if we do nothing with our lives ..."

"And the room with a bed had the gold lock ..."

"Because home is the most important thing." He embraced her tightly. "Your home is in my heart, and you shall live there forever."

Johanna felt the warmth of Roderick's hand pressed into hers.

"Now, my love, you must come with me. We shall marry under the trees, but first, the witch must die."

So, they set out for the home of the forest witch, and when they entered silently, together, Johanna felt a chill run down her spine as the witch looked at them and spewed venomous curses, but she was chair-ridden and could not harm them any further than that.

"Kill her," said Johanna under her breath. "She frightens me so."

"Be patient, my love," replied Roderick. "I will not kill her myself. I have a far better idea." Johanna felt a tug as Roderick pulled her into the room with all of the glittering rings. He removed his black hat with a long, flowing plume and began scooping rings into it. They clattered as they fell in and when he was finished, the hat was filled. The room still contained plenty of rings.

Silently, Roderick and Johanna left the cottage as the witch screamed, "Thieves! Thieves!"

When they were out of her earshot, Johanna turned to Roderick and asked, "How will this thievery help us to destroy her?"

"Trust me, my dear one," Roderick replied. "Now, lead me to the place where you last saw the coach robbers."

By now, Johanna knew her way around the forest very well. She raced through the forest, kicking up leaves as she went, and Roderick clutched his filled hat to his chest tightly as he ran beside her.

Finally, Johanna paused. She looked around and then nodded. "This is the spot."

"Great!" Roderick replied. He bent down to the ground and placed an ornate diamond ring there. Then a couple inches from it, in the direction of the woods, he placed another. Then he set his hat on the ground and reached into his pocket, producing the golden key. He handed it to Johanna. "You must get some rest tonight. Stay hidden, and safe. This will take me all night. In the morning, I will come for you."

"Be careful, my dove," she said, accepting the key and then sinking into his arms.

That night, Roderick waited outside the old woman's house. He saw the glow of the lantern light as the thieves followed the trail of rings he'd laid out for them, and heard the life-ending scream of the old woman as they unloaded their revolvers once more. He smiled as he peered in through the window to see them loading their fingers with jeweled rings ... and howled with delight as he heard a deafening crack, and saw that two new trees stood right where the thieves had been.

Contributors

Dallas Alexander is an Author, a Barista, and a Substitute Teacher. She is the wife of a free-spirited husband and the mother of a soft-pawed dog.

When she isn't writing, she enjoys going out to the movies, doing laundry at her parent's house, visiting her chickens, and making art that involves fire.

Kendall Bartels is a writer from south Florida, where she currently resides after spending some time in Los Angeles.

The author graduated from the University of Central Florida in 2016 with a bachelor's degree in theatre and literature; she acted in a handful of indie films, before returning home to the east coast to pursue her passion of writing.

Kendall was recently offered a contract for her debut novel *Professor Knight*, a romance inspired by Jane Austen's *Pride and Prejudice*, which is set to be released in the fall of 2018.

Currently, the author lives with her amazing family and bald cat, Dobby.

You can find her on social media, like Twitter and Instagram, using her handle @KendallHere

Gene J. Parola

Gene J. Parola, a cultural historian, retired from Koç University in Istanbul, Turkey and returned home to Hawai'i to delve into Island history.

Lehua, Ka'ao a ka Wahine, his Prize Winning Historical Novel, is the first of a trilogy that has kept him in research for most of ten years.

Mr. Parola has been published in two volumes of short stories by Bamboo Ridge Press, *Journal of Hawaiian Literature and Arts* and in the anthology, *Voices from the Universe.* He has written on the revolution in publishing in the Honolulu Star-Bulletin, and for the Island retirees magazine, *Generations.*

He has published two mystery novels *The Devil to Pay,* a seagoing fiction based on a less well-known Kennedy assassination theory, and *Old Sins, New Sinners*, based on his years in the Middle East. He also has three collections of short stories. *Portraits of a Young Artist in Istanbul* from his collection, *The Little American Blonde* won an Editor's Choice Award at AuthorStand. In addition, there are *The Pearl Harbor that Didn't Happen'* and *The Professional* available as e-books.

Mr. Parola is a 'blue water' sailor of five of the seven seas, a wood sculptor, a public speaker, and a grandfather of three. He lives with his author wife, Shirley T. Parola, in Honolulu, Hawai'i.

Leslie D. Soule

Leslie D. Soule received her M.A. in English from National University. She is a scholar, artist, citizen journalist, and martial artist. She has been an established writer for a decade.

What sets her work apart from the pack, is its intensity in dealing with the ultimately personal journey of life and its myriad setbacks and sorrows. Her novels contain a deeply populist, anti-establishment tone, one in which rebellion against the often-authoritarian norm is praised. Her work embraces the outcasts of society—the discarded, the rebels, the people that the magazines forgot to tell you exist.

Readers enjoy Soule's no-nonsense, fast-paced style of writing. She loves to hear from her readers, encourages them to connect with

her on Twitter and to help spread the word
about her work.

Other Anthologies from Zimbell House

The Fairy Tale Whisperer
The Mysteries of Suspense
Garden of the Goddesses
Elemental Foundations
Romantic Morsels
The Steam Chronicles
Pagan
Tales from the Grave
The Adventures of Pirates
Curse of the Tomb Seekers
Travelers
Dark Monsters
On a Dark and Snowy Night
Where Cowboys Roam
The Key
Veil of Secrets
Tournament Games
The Lost Door
Nocturnal Natures
It's an Urban Style of Love
The Neighbors
Date Night
Why? A Collection of Mysterious Tales
The Mountain Pass
River Tales
After Effect
Morsels from the Chef
Ghost Stories
Second Chance
Children of Zeus

A Nymph's Tale

Attack of the Federation

Hades Had a Son

Coming Soon from Zimbell House

Poseidon's Daughter

No Trace

The Dionysus Society

❦

Join our mailing list to receive updates on
new releases, discounts, bonus content, and
other great books from

Or visit us online to sign up:
http://www.ZimbellHousePublishing.com

A Note from the Publisher

How to Thank a Contributor

Dear Reader,

Everyone at Zimbell House Publishing would like to thank you for reading *If I Say No*. If you would like to thank a particular contributor, the best way is to leave a review for them. You may do so by leaving one on our Goodreads page, under the *If I Say No* title, by using the link below and be sure to mention the contributor directly:

http://www.goodreads.com/ZimbellHousePublishing

Why should you leave a review? Reviews help budding authors build their credibility in the book industry. By posting a review on Goodreads or other sites, you help other readers find new authors they may wish to follow, and you never know, your review may end up on an author's website one day.

Friend us on Goodreads:
https://www.goodreads.com/ZimbellHousePublishing

Follow us on Facebook:
https://www.facebook.com/ZimbellHousePublishing/

Follow us on Twitter:
http://twitter.com/ZimbellHousePub